Incarcerated Heart

WOLLO'S SON

Published By
AF&M Publications, LLC

DEDICATION

This novel is dedicated to the #1 Queen in my life - my Mother, Queen Wanda Wollo. Also to the Black Queen who was allowed to introduce her to the world; Queen Selma Moss (May God bless her soul). I also dedicate this novel to my family tree and all those that still believe in me. To the one that helped make my dream a reality – I love you (you know who you are). To my siblings: James, Cherry, Aisha, Chris and Shannon – I love you all more than words can express. Last but not least, my children, I love you all unconditionally.

Contents

ACKNOWLEDGMENTS

All praise and thanks belongs to God for my family, life and for allowing me the ability to orchestrate this book. I also thank God for the people whom I've had the opportunity to cross paths with – past and present.

I thank God for my Mother; Queen, thank you for showing your undying love for me and for truly showing me what a Mother's love is really about – especially when I started 'smelling myself' and stepped outside the teachings you and Mother Dear taught me…thanks! I can never express my gratitude to you for continuing to believe in your bad boy.

I would also like to thank God for a few special people who have remained ten (10) down, and one (1) up with Wollo's Son. Thank you all for not abandoning me, your actions and deeds have shown me that the love you have for me isn't artificial. Know that my love for you is uncut.

1 CHASING DREAMS

It was a cold winter day in Quincy, Illinois. For Bria Lewis it was just another day of hard work and one more night spent all alone, sprawled across her queen sized bed. Besides that, she hated to be the one to go and scrape the ice off the frozen windows of her car and warm it up. This is another reminder for her to purchase an automatic starter to be installed on her 2013 Honda Accord.

She realized by getting an automatic starter for her car, it would at least solve one of her many problems, she wouldn't have to scrape off anymore ice from her car windows in the mornings. After coming up with a solution for one of her problems, she started to think in her mind, what she could do concerning the vacancy she had inside her heart.

After pondering for a few minutes, her thoughts were shot down by the realization that her job demanded too much of her time. Damn, she said to herself - Ooooh Boy! I could truly use some company, some romantic display of affection, a gentle touch of a masculine hard tender sweet kiss that would tug at a woman's heart. And the Lord knows I could surely use some good old fashioned love making. Her thoughts alone were warm enough to melt the winter snow.

Today was no different from any that had come before it. Bria would wake up, take care of her hygiene, fix a quick bite to eat and then hurry off to work.

Bria graduated from Quincy University with an impressive 3.8gpa, earning her a Bachelors of Arts Degree in Journalism. Upon graduating, Bria was hired by one of the top news providers of urban interests. The 411 was a newly comprised magazine that touched on the areas of urban life that the other news providers neglected to deal with.

The company gave Bria the freedom she longed for as a journalist. She had the opportunity to express herself on some very important issues. She took pride in keeping her people informed.

Bria was the epitome of every man's desire. She was educated, sexy, and without any children. For a twenty-seven year old, this was fading fast in today's society. Her five foot six inch, one-hundred thirty pound frame was that of an unblemished perfection that was magnified by the Creator's artistic expression. Her exotic features often got her mistaken for being from the Islands. With her stunning looks and well-proportioned figure, she was the object of every man's fantasy. She had hazel eyes that could pierce the soul along with all the class that could be sold. She would be classified as a sexy intellectual.

After finishing her breakfast of fresh, mixed fruits (strawberries, honeydew, cherries and pineapples) and lightly buttered whole wheat toast, Bria decided that before going to work she would call and holler at her rowdy girl, Lisa.

Placing her dishes in the sink, she made a mental note to remember to pick up some dish detergent, eggs, and a box of fruity pebbles. With the to-do list lodged in memory, Bria grabbed her purse and leather coat before leaving the house.

The sudden change in temperature, once she stepped outside, gave her instant goose bumps and sent chills throughout her body. She wanted so badly to turn around and go curl up in front of her fireplace with a romance novel and a cup of hot chocolate. Her strong will and determination wouldn't allow her to follow through. Bria's bullheadedness drove her ambitions and a day's rest would come with retirement. Until then she would continue to be all work and no play.

Entering the warm sanctity of her car, she managed to retrieve her phone from her purse. Glancing at the screen she noticed that she had missed three calls, one from Lisa, someone from her job, and one unknown. Deleting the missed calls; Bria called Lisa back. Although it was seven-thirty in the morning, Lisa would be up getting ready for work.

Lisa answered the phone chipper as usual with a bubbly tone. "Hello", Lisa said upon answering the phone--"What you doing Wench?!" Bria said sarcastically. "Girl I'm waiting for Rick to finish clearing the ice off my car." "Who is Rick?" Bria asked with concern. Lisa said fallaciously, "Girl, I met him last night over drinks and dinner. Shit, his conversation was good and the brotha is fine as hell, not to mention a sistah was in need!" It's good to know your needs were met by some random stranger, Bria spoke with conviction. "Don't go there girl, you know it's not like that. It's my way of relaxing, there are some of us that still like to be serviced while others prefer manual labor", Lisa stated with hidden intent.

"So what are you trying to say, Ms. Lisa?" Bria spoke in a jazzy, more serious tone. "Shit! All I'm saying is there's nothing wrong with a little wet tongue and steel rod. That's all I'm saying girl", Lisa replied with a preferential undertone.

"Well I hope you enjoyed your wet tongue and steel rod, I have to get to work where you should be. Call me when you get off, heifer." Bria said, while looking at her watch. "Okay, I will, you drive safe out there". Lisa said, before hanging up the phone.

Pulling out of her driveway, she couldn't help but to think about Lisa's remarks. Bria couldn't remember the last time she was in the presence of a man. At least not in a romantic arrangement, let along being on the receiving end of some wet tongue and steel rod, as Lisa put it. With all of her obligations, she just didn't have the time, according to her reason for missing out on the receiving end. Besides, Bria's insecurities kept her hung up on frivolous worries.

Turning off 12th street onto Chestnut Street, Bria was dying to shake the comments of Lisa out of her mind. "Stay focused girl, be strong." She told herself, turning off her subconscious desire to be held close and loved. Coming back to reality, she was amazed that the roads were clean and clear of snow and ice.

She didn't like the winter conditions but being a Midwestern girl, she could handle herself. Tired of chasing her thoughts, Bria turned on the CD player and selected CD #6 (which was one of Trey Songz CD's). She couldn't help but to play her favorite song "Think I Invented Sex." Listening to the crooner seductively describe his sexual prowess only made matters worse for her.

Today would be a light day's work and Bria made a promise to herself that she would pick up the few groceries she needed after work and stop by Poppa Murphy's to get a medium pizza with chicken, onions, bell peppers and mushrooms, which was her favorite.

She wanted so badly to soak in a hot tub of Milk-N-Honey. Her body more than deserved to be pampered. "Tonight will just be me and my toys." She spoke to no one in general.

Exiting her car, she prepared herself for an erotic work environment knowing she would have to make it through the day first.

*****

Lisa waited for her new conquest to come back inside out of the cold winter air. Although Lisa had to be at work by nine, she had a little over one hour to get her last minute quickie.

All she could think about was the many ways "God" was called last night. She could still feel the tingle his tongue sparked throughout her body, on top of the fact he was a sexy hunk of a man who knew how to lay some pipe. She truly thought that she would have broken her thirty dollar acrylic tips if she had dug any deeper into his soft flesh.

Caught up in her freaky little thoughts, Lisa didn't hear Rick enter the room with stealth like sneakiness. His presence was welcomed with a mischievous smile, "are you ready to go woman!?" Rick said in his husky baritone voice. "Not yet tiger," replied Lisa as she turned to face him. Lisa let her eyes wonder over his muscular physique with licentious appraisal.

Wasting no time Lisa provocatively sauntered her way into his arms. The warmth of his body was so inviting and the pressure he applied was soothing. Wrapped in his constricting arms, Lisa exhaled a soft moan of pleasure into his chiseled chest. Listening to the pitter patter of his heart was like listening to the most beautifully sung lullaby.

Lisa felt like a child if only for that moment. The feeling of her comfort was overridden by her desire to be man-handled. She raised her head from his chest so that she could transfer the urgency in her pretty brown eyes. She spoke with subtleness. "Would you mind hooking a sistah up before she goes to work?" Lisa spoke flirtatiously. "I take it this sistah didn't get enough last night." Rick said, allowing himself to play her little game. "I'd say she got hers and then some. It's just that it was so good she wants a little more." Lisa said. "Well you know what they say: what's nice comes twice and three times a charm." Rick said, clearing a loose piece of Lisa's hair from her face.

"Well let's see if we can make this third time the charm," Lisa stated. Rick whisked Lisa off her feet and carried her down the hall to the master bedroom. Laying her softly on the bed, Rick didn't bother pulling back the sheets.

Being that Lisa was scheduled to be at work by nine o'clock she got straight to it, unfastening his pants with the speed and agility of a cheetah. Like a ferocious feline, Lisa pulled down Rick's pants with brute force. Now with more gentleness, she released his semi-erect wonder as she slid his white cotton boxer-briefs down around his thighs. Going for what she wanted; Lisa grabbed an adequate handful of his manhood and worked up a nice and steady stroke, bringing him to a complete erection.

Without haste, Lisa removed every article of her clothing revealing her voluptuous body." Do me right!" Lisa said lying across the bed revealing her sweet spot. Words wouldn't register fast enough for Rick. Going from zero to sixty in six seconds, he was on her like white on rice! "Control me big daddy," Lisa whispered her words with stimulating affects, high off of the excitement she knew that was bound to come. Rick entered her warm velvety center with no regard to remove the rest of his clothing. Morning sex was always Lisa's favorite; and what a good day it was going to be.

*****

As Bria expected it was chaos at work, and she desperately wished Calgon could just take her away. Beginning the work week is always hectic with Monday morning conference meetings and dealing with the diverse mixture of Monday morning attitudes is always tough.

The environment was all but inviting. Even still, Bria loved her job and wouldn't trade it for the world. She has always had a passion for writing. Her ability allowed her to dabble in every genre of creative writing, but her skill was at its best when she expressed herself poetically. This is where her talent flourished. Ever since she was a child, she loved the rhythmic melodies of poetry. She took great pride in entering random contest; where the prize winning often varied in comparison. Some contest, if won, the winner could receive up to five thousand dollars cash, while others would offer full scholarships to aid in advancing the winners love for the craft.

Bria enjoyed being in different contests, even though she always seem to lose way more than she won. It never seemed to deter her from entering the contests anyway; this made her skin a little thicker. She looked upon her losses as temporary setbacks.

At a young age, Bria knew she wanted to go to college and get a degree in writing. She also knew that if she could win the writing contest, sponsored by the Poets & Writers Magazine, it would increase her chance of getting a full four year scholarship. She was determined to win one of the magazine's contests.

In her junior year of high school, she once again entered the Poets & Writers Magazines' contest. The topic for the contest was "Artistic Expression", which allowed the writer free reign to present their uniqueness.

Bria won the contest that year, chosen over thousands of other talented writers. The prize for winning was a scholarship to Quincy University, which would help her expand her love for writing. Though it had only been six years, to Bria it seemed to be a long time ago. It still amazes her to have earned a degree with valor and honor.

Being the first generation graduate of the Lewis family, Bria met the uncertainty with courage. She often reflected back and wondered how she managed to stay focused when many of her friends had dropped out of school, college, or either started having babies.

After finishing school, her plans had always been to write her own columns and ultimately establish her own publishing company.

Immediately after Bria graduated, she was offered an opportunity to fulfill her dream, one which she accepted with no questions asked. She was offered a job to work with a top magazine company called '411', as a writer. The job came with no special treatment offers; but due to Bria's hard work and dedication, she was able to prevail herself through the ranks with stubborn perfection.

After Bria had written a few featured articles in the 411, the company started receiving a lot of buzz from readers demanding more of her. The magazine met their loyal fans demands by offering a daily dose of Bria.

Bria's ambitious ways allowed her to touch home with her followers (this kept her relevant); which remains to be her focal point. She was always able to shed light on social problems that were deliberately ignored by the mainstream media. Bria never failed to bring the "REAL" in reality, it was her slogan.

With her mind lost on the obvious; Bria directed her brain to tune in to as much of the morning conference as was needed. She always managed to come from her fantasy land when the valid points were being addressed. It was a habitual habit that she had mastered. Once the conference had adjourned, Bria felt relieved as she gathered her belongings and headed towards the door.

Being cordial, she exchanged pleasantries with her colleagues in passing. As she was about to exit the conference room, her boss called for her attention. "Miss Lewis, would you mind if I had a word with you?" In a professional tone, Bria replied, "Sure Mr. Sanders, what can I help you with?"

"I am grateful, but I was thinking maybe there was something that I could help you with", Mr. Sanders stated with genuine concern. "What makes you think I need help sir?" Bria shot back, uneasy but stern. "It doesn't take a rocket scientist to figure out that you have something on your mind." Mr. Sanders replied.

"It's nothing serious Mr. Sanders and I must apologize for my absent mind this morning". Bria stated. "No need for apologies, I just wanted to know if it was something serious and if I could help is all." Mr. Sanders spoke as he stood up collecting his materials off the table. "I assure you Mr. Sanders that there is nothing wrong." Bria replied, burying the burden in hopes that no one would find it.

"Well, I'm sure you will figure it out, you always do. By the way, did you have a chance to read the memo that I sent to you; concerning the special we're planning for Black History Month this year?" "Yes, sir, and I will be ready."

Saying their goodbyes, Bria turned and walked towards the elevator. Pressing the down button, she waited impatiently. The elevator chimed when it reached the thirteenth floor. Boarding the lifeless elevator, Bria pressed the button for the sixth floor and then stepped to the rear of the vertical assistant. She then resumed the epic that stood on standby in her mental cinema. All she could think about was the masked man that found great joy in torturing her with pleasure. Every night when she fell asleep he would appear tall, fair toned, and sexy as hell.

The way he devoured her body with his attentive mouth made her purr. Ooooh and the way he would lay his feather soft kisses down the small of her back drove her wild. His scent was intoxicating, one she had smelled before, but she couldn't put a name to it.

When he would draw her near, it was as if he were a soul snatcher, because she was always at a loss of breath. This brother systematically took her through all of R-Kelly's "twelve" steps. A procedure acted out with the sole intent on driving her wild with uncontrollable passion. This would grab her from her dreams many nights, only to find herself lying in her bed alone and moist down in her hidden valley. Nipples awakened by the tenderness of the tender caress. The feeling was instructive, but yet disappointing because it was only a figment of her imagination.

Once the elevator reached her floor, Bria released a great sigh of discontent. Collecting herself she exited the elevator to a circus of raucous, 'business as usual', she said under her breath.

As Bria made her way to her cubicle, she replaced her high heels with a pair of leave at home slippers which happened to be a sore subject upon her being hired.

Mr. Sanders nearly exploded the first time he saw Bria outside of her appropriate work attire. Due to his open mindedness, he agreed with her concerning that the more comfortable a writer, the better the material they would put out. I guess you can say that Mr. Sanders caught on quick. Hell, he even walked around the office in his Ice Cubes, referring to the slippers the actor wore in the movie Boyz N Da Hood.

Once Bria got situated, she entered her password into the computer, unlocking her sacred files. When the screen lit up the 'you got mail' icon appeared, indicating that she had unread emails. Bria scrolled through her menu list then she finally opened her emails. One email was from Lisa who was just checking to see if she had made it to work safely, along with a request for Bria to call her when she had time.

Bria made plans to call Lisa on her lunch break, which was less than an hour away. After reading her messages, Bria closed her emails and began her work for the day.

Getting comfortable in her cushioned chair, Bria settled into its grooves. This was the same chair she'd had since starting with 411. When she sat in the chair, it would shape its form into the contours of her frame. After making one final adjustment, Bria reached over and grabbed her CD case to retrieve her 'oldie but goodie' CD. She knew exactly what she wanted to hear, Ms. Betty Wright. After placing the CD in her player, she went to her favorite jam, 'Tonight Is the Night'. What a compliment to the recent chain of events and not to mention that Bria had been abstinent for about three years. This song on the contrary was definitely intended for her virgin ears.

As the music played, Bria searched to fall into the exact mood and primary feelings that was the root to her driving force. Channeling into the energy that enabled her to always produce top notch material; she was able to finish up on an article that she'd been working on which was due by this coming Friday. Completing the article freed her for the rest of the work day, which brought a great relief.

She could now take a much needed lunch break, although she didn't have an appetite, she could use the fresh air. Besides, it was killing her to know what 'Ms. Lisa' wanted to discuss with her. As Bria prepared to close out her file and log off her computer, she made sure to save the work she had just completed before taking off for possibly the rest of the day.

Grabbing her coat and purse from under her desk, Bria made her way towards the elevator. Before leaving she stopped to inform the secretary that she was leaving and to take messages for her.

Haunted with the thoughts that controlled her mind all morning, Bria was desperate to find a solution that would help her clear her mind. She stepped out into the northern hawk that had cast its remnants throughout the area with a blanket of snow and ice. It instantly caused chills sending sporadic shivers through every muscle she had. Pulling her extremities close in hopes to generate some heat, she took great stride to free herself of the obdurate climate. Mother Nature definitely could be harsh in her cycle.

Accessing her vehicle, there was no time wasted in turning the heat on full blast. After a few minutes she set off for her next destination. Once her body heat reached a level of normalcy, Bria grabbed her phone and dialed Lisa's number. Lisa answered her phone after the second ring, sounding full of anxiety. Trying to resist the urge of having Lisa spill the beans, Bria asked her to meet her at 'The Pier', which was their favorite restaurant. They both agreed on the arrangement before ending their call with pleasant good byes. Bria could only wonder what it was that her girl wanted to talk about; knowing Lisa, who knew!

Arriving to the restaurant before Lisa, Bria went ahead and got seated, while waiting she decided to order her and Lisa a 'Shirley Temple'. Shortly after placing the order, Lisa entered the restaurant looking like an Eskimo with all of her winter gear on. Once Lisa spotted Bria already sitting at the table, she told the hostess that she would be joining her friend that was already seated. Lisa made her way to the table and the two formally greeted one another. Amused by Lisa's appearance, Bria couldn't help but to laugh. "What are you laughing at girl?" Lisa asked curiously. "Oh nothing!" Bria said, trying not to burst at the seams.

"Well, whatever has you tickled pink, I'd sure like to know, so I can have me a laugh too." Lisa replied, intrigued by the silent joke. "Girl it's nothing! It's just that you look like an Eskimo wrapped up all tight like that." Bria said, enjoying a good laugh.

"Forget you wench, a bitch was cold as hell!" Lisa responded with condor.

Removing her coat, Lisa hung it on the back of an empty chair at their table. By doing so, she knew she didn't have to worry about it coming up missing. In today's society one could never be too careful, especially in the neighborhood they were at.

Settling in her seat, Lisa grabbed one of the menus, and started surveying its selections with greedy eyes. "Damn Bri, I'm hungry as hell!" "Well help yourself, this one on me." Bria spoke without looking up from her menu. "You don't have to threaten this sistah with a good time!" Lisa replied.

They both were so focused on reading the menu, they were unaware of the waitress waiting to take their orders; startled by the waitresses unfamiliar voice, Bria and Lisa ran down their orders in unison.

"I'm sorry girl, go ahead." Bria stated. Turning her attention toward the waitress, Lisa ran off her order. "I'll have the braised short ribs with home fries, and a side order of the BBQ baked beans." Lisa said politely. "Will that be a half, or full rack today Mam?" the waitress asked Lisa.

"Are you ready to place your order Miss?" the waitress turned and asked Bria. "Umm, I'll just have a slice of your banana-strawberry pie." Bria stated. "Will that be all ladies?" the waitress asked with a smile. "Yes, that will be all, thank you." Bria and Lisa recited simultaneously.

As the waitress turned to walk away, another waiter approached the table as if rehearsed with the two Shirley Temples in hand. "Here are your drinks ladies. If there is anything I can help you with, please feel free to call me." The waiter insisted with adorable charm. "We're fine for now, thanks though." Lisa spoke, accepting his informal request to flirt. Taking sips of her relishing Temple, Bria got straight to the reason for their gathering.

"So Lisa, what is it that you wanted to talk to me about?" Bria asked, while she continued to sip on her cherry fizz.

"Girl you know that you're my sistah, and I love you." "Oh-no; what is it now Lisa!?" Bria cut her off mid-sentence. "If you would let me speak, I'll tell you. First let me start by saying: I only say this, cuz I feel that you are depriving yourself of happiness that you are so deserving of. I mean look at you girl! You're beautiful, smart, independent, no kids, very caring and on top of all that, you're successful! There are a bunch of men who would kill to have a chance to be with you." Lisa said, in a very motherly tone.

"I appreciate your concern Lisa, but I'm happy, and it doesn't take a man to keep me there. Besides, I don't have time for a relationship right now." Bria replied, trying to conceal the obvious.

"Look at you Bri; you can't even believe your own words." Lisa shot back. "So all of a sudden you're a relationship specialist!? I mean let's be real Lisa; you aren't the ideal romance counselor. A man has no room in your life; just your bed!" Bria said with frustration.

"Bria it's obvious this is a sore subject with you, I'm not picking at you. And you're correct, a man has no place in my life, but you best believe he can share my bed." Lisa stated with a huge smile.

"When the right one comes along, and presents himself to me. That's when I'll deal with any physical needs; until then, it's work, and my vibrator. Bria retorted sternly.

"Okay Bri, I won't harass you, but I know your forearms are strong as hell from your workout with your vibrator." Lisa said, with a hearty laugh.

"Forget you hussy, you got jokes." Bria shot back in her defense.

The mixture of the aromatic medley of herbs 'n' spices led a trail of seduction right to their table. Lisa hoped the invigorating scent was coming from her order; she scanned the room to see if she could spot the waitress coming her way. Like clockwork, the waitress appeared from the kitchen with a platter. Approaching their table, the waitress read off their orders with practiced experience. Leaving the two women to their meals, the waitress went to tally up the tab. They both enjoyed their food; Bria paid the bill and gave the waitress a respectable tip. Bria and Lisa prepared themselves to leave the restaurant as they bundled up just before stepping back out into the winter elements.

Lisa stated; "We have to do this again soon, but my treat." "Call me Bri." Lisa said. "I will!" Bria responded as she was entering her car.

As Bria pulled out of the parking lot, she decided that she would take the rest of the day off from work. Something she hardly ever did, but with Mr. Sanders knowing she was going through something, she would easily be covered.

Reaching in her purse for her phone, she dialed her work number. After a couple of rings the office secretary answered on the other end.

"Hello! This is '411' Magazine, how may I help you?" Michelle, the secretary stated. "Hey girl, this is Bria, have I received any messages? Could you please inform Mr. Sanders that I'm going to take the rest of the day off, I need to take care of some things?" Michelle responded as if she had some type of 'ESP,' (you could use some time to yourself.)

Bria said, to herself; 'Damn! Is it that obvious that I'm going through some things?' "I'll see you tomorrow Chelle." Bri said, before saying bye and hanging up.

"Well, I guess I'll go to the grocery store and get the items I said I would pick up." Bria said, aloud to no one.

After leaving the grocery store, Bria made one more stop to pick up her pre-order pizza from Poppa Murphy's. All that was left for her to do is head home, so she could treat herself to a night of relaxation.

2 CHASING MY DESTINY

Lying back in his bunk, Tywoun stared at the picture clutched in his hand. The photo was the reflections of his daughters Brittani and Elise. It's been eight years and some change since he was picked up by the West Central Illinois Task Force on armed robbery charges. He was sentenced to a sewbuck; which in laments terms meant a ten year sentence. No stranger to incarceration he took his time like a man. It's just this bid here was different from the rest. The smile on the adorable faces resembling his own; is exactly what made this bid different from the others.

The dynamics of his life had changed the day he became a father. He justified his criminal behavior by telling himself that it was for his family. This happens to be what many dope boys irrationally believe. Anything to put a smile on his baby girls' faces was in the realm of possibility.

Scheduled to be released January twelfth, twenty-fifteen, had left him eight and a half hours until he would be granted the freedom he so desperately wanted. Coming home a totally different person than he was in his past life. He was anxious and somewhat fearful of the voyage that was ahead. No matter how many times he told himself he was prepared, the butterflies accompanied with the flatulence took his stomach on a roller-coaster ride; a ride of uncertainty. It is normal to be afraid of the unknown, and outside of the macho bravado he admitted to himself that he was indeed, scared to death. Seventeen out of the twenty-seven years of his life, he has spent in the University of Street Tactics. With a major in 'Hustlenomics' and a minor in 'By Any Means Necessary;' he managed to prevail to the head of his class. Born with the natural ability to lead, respect and influence was a given.

Tywoun grew up on Ninth and Lind streets in Quincy Illinois on the north end of the city. Making poor decisions led him down a road of constant pot-holes and road blocks. Sick and tired of dodging bullets, fake friends and most of all, doing time. He cut all ties to his previous life. It was definitely a test of will versus temptations. The constant pressure and scrutiny only strengthened his resolve. He didn't know how it was going to be done, but somehow he knew he would find answers.

All that mattered to him at this point in his life was being a father to his children. It wouldn't hurt to find a nice woman, settle down and live a normal life. There were so many thoughts running through his mind at this point sleep would be a hard fought battle. Rehearsing exactly what he wanted to say to his baby girls; he went through the motions of their long overdue reunion. He wondered if they would hate him for not being there, or would they even want to see him. Due to the non-communication between him and their mother, he hasn't spoken with nor seen his girls since he'd received his sentence.

Tears filled the lids of his eyes, but were unable to spill over. Trying not to bring pain to this blessed occasion, he placed the photo back under his bunk. Tonight would be the longest night of his life. Dealing with the distraction of regaining his freedom, Tywoun decided to unfold the thoughts that ran rampant through his mind. Reaching for his note book and pen, he began to express himself. Jotting down the rhythm of his heart, he added punctuation to the age old saying: 'Out with the old and in with the new.'

In light of the events in his life present and past, he constructed a master piece entitled, Freedom and Redemption.

Freedom and Redemption

Freedom is only an expression without the right words, or maybe it's the right to take flight and scour the earth like the strongest of birds.

Or, just maybe Freedom is a state of existence that few obtain, free from the shackles of the heart and or mind, making you strong and fearless, but cold, calculating and heartless all at the same time.

If that is Freedom, do I want to strive in that direction? Lacking emotions to respond, the companionship to bond, or the need for affection.

Talking about my dilemma, when these bars, this hard cot should be my immediate concern, but then again, this I know will pass, and yes, time will be wasted, without certain questions learned or asked.

And what if I did obtain Freedom wouldn't 'Redemption' be her closest friend? The only one with a key to unlocking the shackles, unleashing the chains, allowing the soul to make amends.

Allowing the heart to breathe, exhale, and then inhale lost emotions, making it easier for the individual to bond, communicate and dedicate strong devotions.

Or should I say 'Individuals' because there is exemption, especially when there's a debate from within questioning ones

Freedom and Redemption

*****

"Inmate Thomas, Register Number three-zero-one-one-five-zero-seven-four! Step up to the counter to be processed out, please!" Shouted the corrections officer. "Yes Sir, Inmate Thomas, Register Number three-zero-one-one-five-zero-seven-four." He yelled over the noise of the other inmates in the bullpen. Stepping up to the counter, he placed his identification card onto its surface. Standing there patiently; he wanted to answer the formal questions, and listened intently while the correctional officer ran off the list of things to do once he was home.

Not much has changed since his last release from prison. The usual: you have twenty-four hours to report to your local probation office, refrain from using any illegal drugs, and you're not to be around any known felons. The funny thing about it all is while they're running down the list of things to do/not to do, not one time is it mentioned to stay out of trouble. The irony in it all is the penal system hide behind the banner of rehabilitation. When in reality, it's business as usual.

When he was done being processed out, he was then taken in another room in R & D (Receiving and Discharge) to be charged out into a prison issue sweat outfit. Once done there, he was escorted through a long tunnel which in many ways represented a rite of passage. Freedom was on the other side of the door that sat twenty feet in front of him. Trying to remain calm, he commanded his jelly like legs to move as he approached a new life, a new day and most importantly living it a new way.

Stepping out into the cold winter day a free man, Tywoun beamed with delight at the beautiful scenery. Never having time to stop and view nature in its' rawest form, he stopped to soak it all in. Eight and some change behind a brickyard stockade will make the toughest of men stop to smell the roses when given the chance.

Gathering himself, he scanned the parking lot hoping to find someone that thought enough of him to pick him up. The fact was no one would be there. Still something inside of him wished his daughters would be there waiting with open arms. Dealing with the reality of the situation he turned and walked to the prison van. Fighting back the anger swelling inside of him, he placed his faith in seeing his kids again. The institution would be dropping him off at the Amtrak Station. From there, he would be taking the 9:00am train, which would carry him to Quincy at 11:45am – his final destination. There he would take the first step towards a promising future.

*****

Awakened by the tremble brought on by the climax of her dream, Bria laid in her bed numb with sensation. "Not again!" She spoke in disbelief. As it necessary she turned over to see if she had company. With the echo of loneliness, her silent cries fell on deaf ears. On the verge of coming undone, she struggled to calm the rapid beat of her heart. Collecting the frenzy that is her mind. She emerged from underneath of her Ethan Allan comforter, and made her way to the bathroom. A good shower would wash away the sinful lust saturated at the apex of her thighs; but it couldn't wash away the tantalizing memories of her mystery man.

Working up a good lather she caressed the cotton softness of her butter-cream skin. Rinsing clean she made one final spin to make sure she'd gotten all of the soap off her body. Stepping out onto the four inch cherry red floor mat, she thought it would be nice if one of these days she could have a fresh out-the-dryer towel waiting to wrap her wetness into warmth. Suddenly, reality hit her when a breath of air crept up her saddened frame. She wrapped herself forcefully hoping to be shielded from the cool brisk air. After pat drying, Bria applied some cotton-candy lotion and body spray Lisa purchased for her twenty-seventh birthday. She thought to call and greet her best friend. Knowing Lisa, she was probably entertaining this Rick character.

Staring at herself in the life sized mirror hanging from the bedroom door, she critically analyzed every inch; mapping out the beauty of her back. That somehow she could find problems with, like her stomach for example, it could be a little bit flatter; or how about her thighs? They could definitely use more definition. Let's not even speak on her breasts. Lord knows they have fallen since graduating high school. Back then, everything was well put and placed just right. Now, she has sheer grace, that of a ballerina, the beauty of a dove and a heart of pure gold deserving the most intimate of loves.

Pulling herself from in front of the mirror, she went to her closet to find something to wear. Today is Tuesday, which happens to be professional Tuesday. So, she headed to the far back of her closet. She found her coffee and crème Donna Karan business pant suit. Accessorizing her choice of dress, she found her root beer brown Jimmy Choos and matching Dooney and Burke bag. The earth tones were the perfect complement to her flawless complexion. Not wanting to be bothered with her hair; she pulled it into a serious business bun with chop stick hair pins. Making her final adjustments, she flossed and brushed her teeth. When she finished, she applied a light application of juicy cinnamon berry lip gloss to her lips.

Before leaving the house, she remembered to take out the chicken so it would be ready to cook when she returned home. Tonight, she had intentions of eating a nice meal, listen to some music and write some poetry. Knowing Lisa, she would drop by and eat dinner with her. This was something they've done since grammar school. She knew her way around the kitchen well; as for Lisa, she couldn't boil water.

Stepping up to go out into the crisp morning air that chaffed the skin with ease, Bria was happy to see the sun had shone early this morning melting some of the snow. The road more accessible; only to refreeze overnight and cause the roadways to become very dangerous.

Letting her car warm up for a few minutes; allowed her to text Lisa about dinner. Bria planned to cook grilled chicken with sautéed bell pepper and onions over a bed of organic brown rice. Pulling out into the desolate city streets she was motivated to have a wonderful day at work. She promised herself that she would not allow anything to pull her off square, not even her mystery man!

*****

Arriving safely in Quincy a quarter till noon, Tywoun was so excited all he could do was smile. Exiting the train and finding the nearest pay phone; he called for a cab to come pick him up. He paid the cab driver (with the ten dollars gate money he received from the prison officer), to take him to the living assistance program the state offered inmates without a place of residence. Tywoun studied the apartment building, and was satisfied knowing the program had no resemblance of a penal institution. The last thing anyone wanted to see after being released from jail is anything related to jail.

Tywoun entered the building and followed the instructions on the sign. He walked down the hall and hung a left. The tidy office that greeted him was occupied with an elderly woman by the name of Ms. Fletcher. Ms. Fletcher reminded of him of some one's sweet grandmother. Getting business out the way, she ran down the rules of the program.

"Well Mr. Thomas, this is the 'Fresh Start' program. I run the program in conjunction with the state, to house individuals upon their release from prison with no place else to go. I want to acknowledge that we all make mistakes, no one is perfect. Some take longer to learn its' lessons than others. Honey, I'm telling you I'm not your Parole Officer (PO), the law nor am I here to cause you any discomfort. I allow all my tenants to conduct their lives on their own terms. All I ask is don't have the people (referring to the police), coming to my place of establishment. You do that and we'll get along just fine. Now, I know you have some catching up to do. Here's your set of keys. You'll be on the second floor, room number twenty-eight; which is a one bed efficiency, but in good condition. Before I forget, rent is due on the first. If for any reason you need an extension due to unforeseen circumstances, I will do my best to work with you. And Son, please do yourself some good; stay out of trouble." Ms. Fletcher said so peacefully.

"Yes Mam!" Tywoun replied respectfully. Turning to exit the office, he held much respect for Ms. Fletcher, and he told himself he wouldn't let her down. Reaching the stairway he rushed to see his new apartment. Opening the door to this new sanctuary, his first thoughts were this is doable. It may not be the Ritz Carlton, but it sure beat a 5'7" cell any day! Counting his blessings, he was already laying out the design for his new place. Stepping in and conducting a formal tour, he was pleased overall.

Finding the bedroom, he gazed at the standard size bed enthralled in the center of the room. Laying his bag of property on the bed; he searched for the phone number to call and inform his PO that he'd made it to the 'Fresh Start' program. He also needed to get clearance to leave the house. After getting the consent need, he made no hesitation to move around. Making a mental note that he was to be back at the house at 2:30pm tomorrow to meet with his PO; he left the apartment.

There was nothing better than commanding one's own life. As he walked down the block he just took in the view. Appreciating the exquisiteness of life's down played significance. One step after the other led him to a familiar neighborhood. The setting was all too familiar, yet he felt like a stranger in a new land. Besides the few passing cars, the area was all but abandoned, which was normal behavior for Mid-westerners in the winter. Mostly everyone was laid up either with their families or someone on the side. Hoping to come across someone he knew from his previous life, he strolled without any specific destination. Looking at the deterioration in the equity of his old neighborhood, it crushed him to see the destruction brought on by the presence of the crack rock. Its' venomous sting spread poison with every bag or vial sold. One thing that would forever remain was the twenty-four hour, seven days a week traffic to the dope buildings. That littered the North end like discarded waste throughout every city in America.

Passing by D&D; a tavern turned everyday hang out spot, would turn a lead on the where a bouts' of his children. Exiting the cold and entering the invitation of warmth, Tywoun scanned the radius of customers enjoying their early afternoon drinks. Just when he thought it was no use; coming from the restroom was an old acquaintance he knew very well.

"Ty-Ty is that you my Nigga!? What's da demo, ALLWELL!" This brother shouted, disrupting the monotony of the atmosphere.

"It's Tywoun now Shyheed, just Tywoun", he spoke calmly. "Damn! Why you dropping governments in dis bitch?" Shyheed retorted unaware of Tywoun's change. "I don't mean to offend you; I ask to be called by my earthly." Tywoun stated emphatically.

"What dem people do to you in there my nigga? Don't tell me dey broke you. Not killa Ty!" Shyheed demonstrated physically signaling the barrels of two guns.

"People change brother," Tywoun said. "What happened to two guns up?" Shyheed said disgruntled. "Shyheed the person you knew no longer exists. Don't get me wrong, he's still in there somewhere." Tywoun stated.

"Whatever nigga – you still Ty-Ty, Mr. Two Guns Up. You can save dat change shit for someone don't know no better. Nigga what you drinking? Remy, Henni or what you want some orange juice?" Shyheed said with sarcasm.

"That's alright – what I really need is to find out where Sharice and the girls are staying now. Can you help me?" Tywoun asked with a gleam of hope in his eyes.

"You mean to tell me dat all the time you was on lock Shorty hasn't written you? Not even about your seeds?" Shyheed sarcastically implied. "You really don't know what's good do you?" Shyheed asked Tywoun.

"Naw brother, I don't know what's good", Tywoun stated sternly. "B-love check dis out, since you got popped by da roams; ya babies mom been out here wild as hell." Shyheed said.

Hearing the news was not shocking for him to bear. It's pretty much regular now days. The man doing whatever it is he wanted, but as soon as he catches a bid the woman steps out to get her row off while he's down. The only concern was how his kids were doing. He honestly didn't care about anything else.

"Let's hit some corners," Shyheed said, downing the rest of his drink. Approaching a fresh off the lot 2015 Pineapple Passion candy print Chevy Tahoe, Tywoun knew that this beauty was a reward of some smokers last little bit of pocket change. Getting in on the passenger side he was hesitant at first. He definitely didn't want to get pulled over with Shyheed, not knowing if he was riding dirty.

"You dirty?" Tywoun asked cautiously. "No brother, you're straight – I most definitely wouldn't put you in harms' way." Shyheed replied.

Feeling at ease, Tywoun set his fear to the side and entered the luxury of ostrich gut interior. The two of them rode through the city and discussed what took place in his absence; which was the usual come home topics. Who's getting money, who's snitching, who fucking who and the unlucky souls that had gotten bodied. After making a couple of stops to pick up money owe to him, Shyheed fumbled a wad of big face one hundred dollar bills, counting out twenty-five hundred and separated it from the rest of the money.

Extending his hand, he gave Tywoun a strong grip handshake as he gave him the bundle of cash. "I can't take your money." Tywoun said, prideful. "That's da Ty I remember, too proud for a hand out. Look homie this ain't charity. Take this money if not for you, for your shorties." Shyheed insisted.

Their eyes locked in a moment of age old understanding between two friends. "I owe you my dude", Tywoun said. "It's nothing, tomorrow I'm taking you shopping to get your gear up." Shyheed replied.

Pulling in front of the Ninth Street projects brought back so many memories for both men. Not understanding why out of all places to stop, Tywoun waited for Shyheed to explain. "Ty, you sittin' a few feet from your lil' ones", Shyheed said.

Feeling as though his lungs were constricting, Tywoun just stared out the passenger side window. Hit with a sudden fit of stage fright he sat in his seat frozen in time. For so many days and nights he played out this very moment in his mind. He'd rehearsed what he would say over and over again. Now, it was as though he never spoke one word before.

"You'll be alright Nigga, just be you." Shyheed assured him. As much as he believed his words, he was still terrified. His kids were only a few months old when he was taken away. They were now eight years old. He only had one baby picture of the twins so he was left with only his imagination. Imagining what they would look like, or who for that matter; him or their mother.

"I'm ready!" Tywoun chanted. "Go meet your babies Nigga, dey waited long enough to see your ugly face. Na, for real though, dey need you my dude." Shyheed said, trying to settle the noticeable tension in Tywouns' face.

As he exited the vehicle, he gave thanks to his friend. Walking up to the apartment door was the longest walk of his life. With nothing but a door standing in front of him and his girls, he felt warm despite the cold outside temperature. He stood at the door for a moment as he listened to the laughter and movement on the other side.

"Knock on the door," Tywoun said to himself. Pulled from his thoughts by the sudden opening of the door. He was face to face with his babies' mother. The color drained out of her beautiful face. Standing there in an awkward silence, the two of them searched for the words to say in one another's eyes.

"How you doing Sharice?" He spoke, breaking the silence. "Wh, wh, when did you get out!?" Answering his question with a question. "Listen Sharice, I don't mean to inconvenience you or what you may have going on in your life, but I want to see my kids." He said. "I don't have a problem with that, but I have company coming over in about an hour. Can you make it quick?" She stated bluntly.

Trying to remain calm, Tywoun swallowed his anger and entered the apartment. Finding a spot to sit he waited patiently. Hollering for the kids to come into the living room, Sharice just stood there agitated.

"Yea, Momma!" The two of them said. "There's someone here I want you to meet." Sharice replied. Entering the living room the two girls were fixed on this stranger sitting on their love seat. "Momma who dis man is?" one of them asked. "Brittani and Elise, this is Tywoun Tyrell Thomas, your father." Sharice answered. "I thought you said we don't have a daddy, Momma!?" Brittani said with puzzlement across her face.

"Girl hush!" Sharice quickly scolded her. Tywoun was very angry at that statement, but managed to remain calm. The only thing that mattered was his children. "Are you really our daddy?" Elise asked, with a bashful demeanor. "Yes, baby." Tywoun answered.

"Where you been at?" Brittani asked. "If you two will allow me, I would like to come and get you after school tomorrow. I have something special planned and I promise I will explain everything then. Ok? That is if it's okay with your mom." Tywoun stated, while looking at Sharice with pleading eyes.

"Well, I guess!" Sharice responded courtly. After a brief moment of conversation their meeting was disrupted by Sharice's reminder about her expected company. Respecting her wishes, Tywoun said his goodbyes and made arrangements to pick the girls up after school the next day. As he was heading for the door, he paused to thank Sharice for allowing him to see his kids.

"You don't have to thank me," Sharice said. Leaving the apartment, he was called back by the girls. Turning to see what it was they wanted, Brittani said "you promise you gone be here to get us tomorrow, and you not gone leave us no more?" "Tywoun looked at his girls with awe in his eyes and said, "Baby I promise I will be here and you don't have to worry about me leaving. I'm not going anywhere." "Well, we gone be waiting." Brittani said with new found happiness in her young voice. Rushing their daddy they locked in a warm embrace that tore at his heart. The feeling was unexplainable! Squeezing both of them in a giant bear hug, he fell to his knees to marinate in the moment. "I knew you would come back daddy." Elise spoke softly.

"Come in here and close that door, you letting all my heat out." Sharice hissed. Bye Daddy, I love you!" Brittani said. "Me too! Daddy!" Elise seconded. "I love you too, babies." Tywoun responded feeling the tears well up in his eyes. On his walk back to the 'Fresh Start' building, he couldn't help but to smile. Tomorrow will be a good day and he planned to enjoy every minute of it.

*****

Capping off a long day's work, Bria came home to a peaceful arrangement. After taking a relaxing hot shower; she changed into a comfortable pair of broken-in sweat pants and a high quality thermal top. Before she got started on tonight's dinner, she called Lisa and ran off a short to do list before she arrived.

Retrieving her crystal set of wine glasses; she popped the cork of an excellent bottle of Pinot Grigio and helped herself to a delicate portion of the pungent blend. It was her way of dulling the edge after a chaotic day.

Grabbing the remote to her 52" plasma flat screen, she turned to the R&B channel provided by her satellite provider. Greeted by the mellow groove of Teddy Pendergrass, she thought of the recent passing of the man, the myth, the legend wishing peace until the soulful maestro.

With the mood set just right, Bria prepared a gourmet meal. As if she was built with a sixth sense, Lisa stepped in the door stomping her boots clean of snow seeming to know the exact time to arrive. The ladies exchanged greetings while Bria continued to plate her magnificent creation. Lisa helped herself to a glass of wine. Snapping her fingers to seductive rhythms of Teddy P; she was taken back to her childhood. Where she used to see her parents slow dancing to the melodic groove.

"Girl, this brings back so many memories." Lisa said, stepping in the name of love. "Tell me about it!" Bria spoke with affirmative denotation.

The two women enjoyed themselves over conversation, good drinks and an even better meal. A few hours had passed and time was calling for this evening to end. With concern, Bria offered Lisa her vacant guest bedroom. Not wanting her to drive under the influence in the winter conditions. Seeing as how the sun shown all morning melting the snow, the roads would be slick with ice.

"Bri, I ain't drunk! Hell, I only had two glasses of wine." Lisa shot back. "Lisa you know you don't need to be out there like that with the roads all icy." Bria said, pleading her case. "Girl, you tripping! Besides, I can't stay tonight because I promised Rick I'd pay him a visit." Lisa stated with fact.

"Well, you be careful and call me so I'll know you made it there." Bria said. "You have a good evening Bria, I enjoyed the meal. The next one's on me, ok?" Lisa stated, walking to the door. "Now you know you can't cook," Bria replied jokingly. "Forget you hussy, I'm getting better." Lisa said, sad fully.

Stopping at the door for a brief hug and final goodbye, the two of them parted ways. Feeling the chill of the night air brought a cataclysmic eruption of shivers throughout Lisa's body. "Hey Lisa!" Bria shouted. "Yea!" Lisa responded. "You sure been seeing a lot of this Rick character." Bria said nosily.

"What's nice comes twice, and three times a charm!" Lisa shouted laughingly as she remembered the phrase Rick had coined. "Am I seeing a romantic engagement evolving?" Asked Bria. "Now girl you know that'll never happen." Lisa said in a serious tone. "Never say never!" Bria spoke through the chatter of her teeth.

"Bye Bri!" Lisa said, before finally getting into her car. Closing the door, Bria adjusted the gauge on the thermostat. Smelling the scent of heat coming from the ventilation duct, steadied the beat of her frosted heart. She started picking up the remains left in the kitchen. After twenty minutes, she had washed the dishes, wrapped the leftovers and placed them in the refrigerator. Turning off the television, and the kitchen lights, she recovered the full bottle of fermented grapes and her empty glass. Heading to her bedroom; Bria sat gingerly at the desk in her room.

Pouring her a glass of wine, she opened her journal to make her daily entry. Pen in hand, Bria expressed the feelings her heart perpetuated. Following the strides of her inner sanction, she was pleased with the night's entry. The cultivating of her mind allowed her to translate exactly how she felt.

Placing her pen back into its holster; she read aloud the piece which was appropriately titled:

Somewhere In My Heart
Somewhere in my heart I smile at the little girl who holds onto the hopes of a better tomorrow.
Somewhere in my heart I smile at a tomorrow that's filled with sunshine…entrenched with thoughts of a love that's all mine.
Somewhere in my heart she has blossomed into a full grown woman…a woman who does not believe in fairytales…but she sits and contemplates the arrival of her Prince Charming.
Somewhere in my heart I smile at the joy that fills my soul…I smile at the rush of life that passes me on a crowded street…I smile cause when I smile it makes my heart skip a beat…I smile somewhere in my heart because there you will forever be…
Somewhere In My Heart

Satisfied with the outcome of her journal entry, she drank the last bit of wine before retiring to her bed. Lying under the spell contrived by the authentic concoction, her mind traveled to a place where intimacy was bliss; accompanied by the presence of her mystery man as her mind journeyed forward. Her body heat activated with the escalating rise kindled by his fire; and ooooh was this brother hot! Never appearing the same way, he unfolded his tricks of the Tantric Arts every way imaginable sending Bria's mind, body and soul searching for his pleasures.

Undressing to nothing but a long tee shirt, she went to her secret stash to summon her trusted toy. "O, what the hell! I'm not going to let him have all the fun." She said to herself, referring to the seducer that continued to control her mind.

Bringing herself too many joys, Bria concluded her night with an encore of convulsions. Sleeping like a baby, she slept well into the morning. Determined to feed the hunger she perceived as pent-up frustration, she began to plan for this must have occasion.

3 UNBINDING THE CHAINS

Lisa couldn't remember the last time she was held this way. It was the warmest embrace. The security she found in this man's arms was reassuring, yet it made her fearful. Fear of the unknown; of being hurt; and mostly, of the feelings he provoked inside of her. Being able to withstand the charm of a man is what gave her strength. This is how she maintained her independence. She believes that once a woman makes the man aware of their infatuation for them, the woman becomes submissive. This was one thing she was not.

She prides herself on being "Every Woman". A woman that embodies intellect, style, and class. Self-sufficient from the demands of a man. She would tell herself, 'Once you let a man in – you invite hurt and pain as well'. This is how she managed to protect her heart.

Usually she would get what she wanted out of a man and split. But this Brother here that lay beside her so peaceful and serene, was a piece of work. He complimented her on all the important things. He truly valued her opinion; no decision was made without her input. The Brother sure knew how to please a woman. He brought the thunder with the rain. Most importantly though, was that he made her feel as if she was the only woman on earth. Even for a woman such as herself, that made her feel good.

Rolling over in his masculine arms, she ogled deep into his handsome face. Feeling the separation, he reacted by pulling her near. The surge of energy that pulsated throughout her body was erotic. She gladly surrendered her being to this gentle giant. The satisfied expression on his face was adorably cute. It left her to wonder could a man have that much adoration for one woman as was displayed across his face. The thought was rattling and jarred her out of her thoughts.

Trying to shake them out of her head, she was flustered by their obstinate portrayal. She couldn't, nor would she open herself up to fall in the pit of love. Regardless of how he made her feel, she would not relinquish her heart to him. Nope, it was totally out of the question, and she was having none of it.

"Lisa, is there something wrong, am I holding you too tight?" Rick said below a whisper with sleep heavy in his tone.

"No, baby I was just yawning", Lisa said convincingly.

See, this was exactly what she meant. Soon as she professed her infatuation for him, not even verbally, but in the chambers of her mind, she became submissive. Not the one to bite her tongue, Lisa couldn't understand why now. With her mind negating the transmissions coming from her heart, she contemplated the happiness that would await her on one hand. The stability of a steady man, the bashful moments will occur between the two. The satisfaction of his sexual superpowers, and who knows the irreplaceable memories of a future family. Then on the other hand, you had the heartache and pain.

No amount of convincing would outweigh the risk of being hurt. There was no need to even fool herself. She know what she had to do, get rid of him ASAP! There was no other way. It was too risky, and she refused to be hurt.

'Not again', she told herself trying to get a few hours of sleep before the sun came up.

4 CHAINS OF HOPE

Awakened by the hum of a vacuum, Tywoun was all smiles this morning. Nothing could replace the elation he harbored for being alive this very morning. It's been so long since he smelled the scent of carpet freshener.

It was 6am which gave him enough time to take a shower and stop by McDonalds to pick up the girls something to eat.

Stepping out of the shower, he lathered his 6'1" frame with Vaseline Intensive Care Lotion. The years of exposure to the chemically harsh water of the penitentiary made him dependent to the skin moisturizer. Clumsily he doctored an adequate amount of Old Spice Deodorant. Staring at himself as he brushed his pearly whites, he honestly could see the maturity brought on by his change. Finished with his hygiene, he got dressed in his prison issued sweat suit and commissary bought Classic Reeboks; making notice to buy himself some clothes.

Leaving the apartment, he greeted the custodian who handled his daily duties without a care. Seeing that this was the attitude he must foster to be successful, he noted that it's not about a fast flip – it was all about being able to provide for his family.

Reaching the ground floor, he spotted Ms. Fletcher rearranging the main office. Stopping to pay his respects, he about scared the daylights out of the elderly woman.

"Son, you'll give an old woman like me the heebie-jeebies creeping up on me like that!" Ms. Fletcher said clenching her heart as she caught her breath.

"I didn't mean to startle you, I apologize. I just wanted to stop in and tell you 'Good Morning", Tywoun said apologetically.

"Good morning honey, how was your first night home?" she asked.

"It was blessed. I found where my babies are staying, so it was blessed", Tywoun replied grinning from ear to ear.

"Well that's good. You make sure you do right so you can be here to raise them babies."

"I plan to Ms. Fletcher. I've missed so much time that I can't afford to miss anymore", he spoke with infallible certainty.

Saying his good-byes, he walked out into the blistering cold of the seasonal cycle. Covering up his ears with his stocking cap, he entered the clear streets as he made his way to Mickey D's. It was every bit of four feet of snow on the ground. Making his way through the oncoming traffic, his destination was only five blocks down the road. After ordering their breakfast, he noticed he was making good time.

Running the order off to him, the attendant at the cash register totaled up the price.

"That'll be $17.20 sir", the employee stated.

Taking his order into his arms, he secured a firm grip of the cup holder that bounded their soft drinks. Trotting through the slush filled streets, he made it to his family's apartment in the projects in about five minutes.

Knocking on the door, he was accosted by Sharice who appeared to have been up already. Helping himself to the warmth that grabbed at his cold body, he then made his way to the kitchen and placed the bag of goodies that reeked of delicious goodness on the table.

"Are the girls up?" He asked Sharice with enthusiasm. "No, I was just about to get them up and ready for school", Sharice said. "I stopped to get y'all something to eat", he stated as he arranged a breakfast of sausage, eggs with cheese, fluffy flapjacks, and orange juice.

He preferred to cook a home cooked meal, but this would have to do for the moment. Perhaps tonight he could fix his famous pot roast, carrots and potatoes. "I'll go wake them up", Sharice spoke in a grateful tone. As she turned to leave, Tywoun sat down, ready to eat breakfast with his family for the first time. Surveying the room, he could tell she'd been cleaning. The good ol' smell of Pine-Sol heightened his senses. "Daddy! Daddy! You came back just like you said", Brittani said as she rushed into his open arms. "Yea Dad, you kept your promise! You sure did", Elise spoke with her childlike sass. "I brought you something to eat before you go to school this morning", he spoke lovingly while scooping them up into his free arm. Kissing them both on their foreheads, he set them back down to tend to their morning meal. Joining in the festivities, he motioned for Sharice to join them.

Reluctant at first, she succumbed to the invitation.

After they'd eaten and were dressed, he bundled the girls up in their winter coats. Refusing to put their stocking caps on out of fear of messing their hair up, he couldn't help but to notice Sharice and the kids. Not saying two words to Sharice as they were leaving, he told his children to go and give their mom a hug and kiss. "Bye momma, I love you!" Brittani said. "Me too!" shouted Elise. "I love you too babies", Sharice recited joyfully.

Wrapping the scarves tightly around their necks and zipping them up past the mouth, Tywoun and the girls set off for the bus stop. Revealing his plan to take them shopping brought a Kool-Aid smile across their cherry-red faces. The bus arrived ten minutes after their arrival. Lost in the company of one another, the sub-zero temperature wasn't even recognizable.

Seeing them off, he reminded them to be ready at 4:00pm. This gave him enough time to meet with his probation officer. In the meantime, he would make rounds and look for employment.

*****

Bria was full of vigor this morning. Everything seemed to be perfect. Wednesday was Open Mic Night at the Poets' Corner, which was a local lounge where artists could display their love for spoken word. Tonight she plans on performing some of her new material. If everything goes right, she hoped to find a decent man to help relieve her sexual frustration. No strings attached, no feelings involved, just one night full of unadulterated passion.

It was hump day at work. That meant lunch would be catered and all articles were due by the end of the day. Being a workaholic gave her the advantage of staying ahead.

Sitting in a hot tub of bubbles, she prepared herself for tonight's adventure. It was definitely out of character to indulge in her lower self, but tonight she would allow her inner-freak to have some fun. 'Lisa does it all the time, how hard could it be?' she asked herself.

After getting dressed, she ate a small meal before she headed to work. Not able to focus on much of anything, the reels of her mind played out numerous scenarios. She saw herself getting on stage and winning the audience with her new piece called "Suggestion". Hoping her words would seduce the ears of the man with the ability to read between the lines.

It's been so long since the last time, she didn't even know if she still had it, whatever that "it" was. One thing was certain, she would soon find out. She pictured passion untamed, wild with ecstasy.

5 MAKING THINGS RIGHT

After meeting the parole agent, Tywoun made final preparations before leaving the apartment. Going to his stash spot, he pulled out ten crisp one hundred dollar bills from the stack. Placing the rest of his money back in his hiding place, he grabbed his coat on the way out the door. He stopped to ask Mrs. Fletcher if she would take any messages pertaining to employment opportunities for him. "Don't you worry child, Nanna Fletcher will take care of it. You just go on now and enjoy this time with them babies, you hear?" "Yes ma'am – thank you Mrs. Fletcher."

"Alright sugar be safe, and wrap them lil ones up, they'll catch the death of pneumonia out there." "Yes ma'am."

Peering up at the mahogany cuckoo clock stationed on the west wall, it read three forty-five pm. This would give him more than enough time to make it to the girls' house where he would wait for them to arrive. The chill in the air cut like a knife, and the wind blew like salt in an open wound. 'Man this hawk is biting', I could sure use a car right now. I have to work on getting one once I get a job", he thought to himself. Crossing the four-way intersection at Twelfth and Chestnut, he spotted Shyheed's candy paint Tahoe at the Fast Stop gas station. Cutting through traffic, he met him at the door.

Exiting the filling station with some orange juice and a box of cigarillos in one hand, and on the phone with what sounded like some random woman of the day, with the other. "Aye hold up shortie. TyTy – I mean Tywoun, what it is my ninja?" "I was just on my way to pick up Brittani and Elise and take them shopping. Can you give us a ride out that way? I want to grab them a few things since I just missed Christmas and their birthday.

After that, we'll probably hit the arcade up before grabbing something to eat. So you don't have to stay." "Since I was going to take you shopping anyway, I'm a step in with y'all. Then you can call me when you're finished. Where you trying to eat at?" "I was thinking Papa Johns." "Aw I'm there, that's my spot!"

The two of them entered the warmth of the idle truck as it sat there purring like a kitten. Left to the sounds of Lloyd Banks & Jules Santana's street banger "Beamer, Benz, and Bentleys", Shyheed carried on with the philly who was enticing him to come over and lay pipe to her with an explicit display of forbidden acts. Turning off Chestnut onto Ninth Street, the projects were a ghost town. Time had definitely changed in the last eight years. When Tywoun was last home, the projects were tippin hard twenty-four seven. Rain. Hail. Sleet. Snow. Since then, the feds had grabbed almost the entire projects on conspiracy charges, leaving a deserted site of scatter cities. Tywoun didn't like that his guys Ra-Ra, Dinkles, No Limit, Nafi and Day-Day had fallen to the injustice of the blindfolded broad holding the disproportioned scale. Although he could appreciate that his kids didn't have to live in that type of environment. When things got better, he promised himself, he would move Sharice and the girls into a nice house out passed the mall. This was where all the do-good people lived.

The clock on the interior wall indicated ten past four. Before he could get out of the car, Brittani busted out the door with Elise on her trail, shouting with excitement...

"Daddy! Daddy! Daddy! "Hey, there's Daddy's two little princesses! You two ready?"

"Yea we ready Dad", Brittani said. "Yea Dad we been waitin. Sure did!" Elise spoke with her classic spunk. "What I'm gone do with you and all that sass lil one?" he questioned with a smile.

"I don't e-ven kn-ow!" Elise said, dragging her syllables. "Mom says she is a hot mess Daddy". Brittani teased. "And what's she say about you?" he asked. "She told me one time I be actin like you. Do you think I act like you Dad?" Brittani questions. "From what I've seen, you do act like me baby girl", he said. "What about me Daddy?" Elise cut in. "Definitely your mother", he answered.

Scooping the two of them up, he spotted Sharice standing in the doorway watching the father-daughter banter between the three. Making eye contact briefly he could feel the void, the distance between them, he knew that these acts had to be overcome for the sake of family.

"Do you plan on feeding them? I only ask so I know if I should make dinner or not", Sharice stated. "I was thinking pizza. How does pizza sound girls?" he asked.

"Yea – Pizza!" they sang.

"Can I have pepperoni on mines Daddy?" Elise asked.

"Ooh-yea Dad pepperoni!" Brittani seconded.

"Pepperoni it is! You want me to grab you anything while we're out?" he asked.

"You can get them some milk for cereal in the morning", she said.

Saying their good-byes, they entered the truck. Tywoun made sure the two of them were strapped in their seat belts. Satisfied with their safety, they set out for the Quincy Mall.

"Hey girls, say hi to Uncle Shyheed", he said.

"Hi Uncle Shyheed!" they said in unison.

"Hey nieces!" Shyheed spoke, pulling the phone from him ear.

The kids erupted in joy when they spotted the Quincy Mall sign. It made Tywoun's heart swell to know their joy. Just to experience it was a blessing. It was an experience he would never jeopardize again. Ever!

Inside, the kids pulled him in a million directions.

"Go ahead, spend this time with your shorties. I got you", Shyheed said.

From K.B. Toys to J.C. Penny; Create-A-Bear to Kids Foot Locker; where they led – he followed. Their young hearts were content and overjoyed to be on a shopping spree with their Dad; who was just as pleased. Whatever they wanted, he provided, no questions. The three of them zigzagged and crisscrossed the entire mall, laughing and enjoying themselves along the way.

After an hour had passed, they had accumulated so many bags, they had no more room on their arms to carry anymore. Tywoun searched the crowd for Shyheed so he could take the merchandise out to the truck; spotting him seated in front of Annie's Pretzels eating a sweet glazed raisin pretzel.

The aroma lured the kids like a tune from the Pied Piper.

"Ooh Daddy can we share a pretzel? Can we?" Brittani pleaded.

"Please Daddy! They're my favorite", Elise chimed in.

"Let me take the bags out to the truck first. After that, we can go to the arcade room, ok?"

"You the best Dad in the world", Elise spat.

This was exactly the turn out he was hoping for. To think, he had feared their not wanting to see him. He cursed himself in silence at the absurdity of the thought.

After dropping off the bags, he returned to the food court where the kids were grilling Uncle Shyheed with a hundred questions. With a look of relief on his face, Shyheed was grateful to see Tywoun had returned.

"You got a handful here man", Shyheed observed.

"What you two doing driving your Uncle crazy?" he asked.

"Dad, Uncle Shyheed is funny", Brittani replied.

"Yea he silly Dad", Elise seconded.

Ordering the pretzel he promised, the three of them devoured a cinnamon pretzel with a side of icing. Once done, they went to the arcade where they wore their little legs out playing "Dance, Dance Revolution". From there they shot some baskets, and tried to win the items in the claw machine, to no avail. Before leaving, the three had stopped to take some pocket photos, where they took a gang of silly photos together.

Leaving the mall, they all worked up a ginormous appetite. You could hear it in the growl of their bellies. Not having eaten anything since breakfast, Tywoun felt a bit faint as well.

Wasting no time, Shyheed escorted them down Broadway to Papa Johns' next to the Liquor Depot. Tywoun and the girls had hurried into the pizza parlor while Shyheed stopped by the Liquor Depot to get a fifth of Remy and lime juice before joining them.

Enjoying a large pepperoni pizza, the four of them smashed the entire pie. Over dinner, Tywoun had learned so much, and openly shared the mistakes of his youth. He can say that Brittani was a mature eight year old. Her favorite color was red; favorite foods were pizza and tacos; one day she had plans to sing like Keisha Cole, and wanted to finish school so she can become the next Soledad O'Brien.

Elise, on the other hand, was more of a fire starter, which wasn't surprising. Her favorite color was sky-blue, and her favorite foods were pizza and fried chicken. She wants to play for the L.A. Sparks and be the next Candace Parker; she was definitely a tomboy.

After sharing themselves, all was forgiven. It was now nine pm and time to get them home and ready for bed.

On the ride home, Elise had fallen asleep, while Brittani was hanging on by a thread. Carrying the two of them in the apartment, he got them dressed and ready for bed. After saying their prayers, the girls scurried to their beds. Tywoun tucked them in and gave them good night wishes.

"Good night Dad. Thank you", Brittani spoke, weighed with sleep.

"Good night Daddy. Thank you", Elise said lazily.

"Good night and sweet dreams. I'll be here in the morning, ok."

"Ok" in chorus.

Downstairs, Sharice was in the living room going over the assortment of gifts.

"You didn't have to buy them all this stuff Tywoun."

"I wanted to do something nice for them."

"Just keep in mind, money can't raise them, and thanks for the milk."

"No problem. We must work together right?"

"That's what seems to work."

"Good night Sharice. I'll be here in the morning to walk them to the bus stop."

"You know you gone spoil them. Don't start something you won't finish."

On his way to the truck he couldn't help but think deeper into Sharice's statement, "Don't start something you won't finish." The pain he felt was brought on not by her words, but by the disappointment caused by abandoning his family and irreplaceable responsibilities. He knew trust will be earned, even within himself.

Once Tywoun got back into the truck with Shyheed, he displayed his game face, presenting a cool demeanor. Shyheed was on the phone still listening to the sexual verses of this horny dame. His arousal was evident in the groping of his male member. Placing his little Jezebel on hold, he looked over at his passenger.

"Look at you nigga. You still weak over baby momma cute ass."

Thinking to himself, Tywoun thought he couldn't be more wrong.

"It ain't like that brah. I didn't hold up my end of the bargain. Besides that, it's been eight and some change. We don't even know one another no more. This way will be the best for the both of us. That way we can focus strictly on being Mom and Dad. You dig?"

"No question. Well since you ain't digging baby momma, step out with me tonight. You still do your poetry thing?"

"Yea – why, what's good?"

"It's this new lounge called Poet's Corner on Eighteenth and Chestnut. It be cracking on Wednesday night from eleven til two in the morning. Plus tonight is Open Mic night. You down?"

"I have to hit up the shower and get dressed first."

"That's cool, we have time. I'm gone drop you off, go bust shorty down, and I'll pick you up before eleven."

Grabbing the large bag of clothes and shoe boxes, Tywoun got prepared for tonight's event. He had little over an hour to get ready and wait for Shyheed's return. Fresh out the shower, he examined the new outfits sprawled across his bed paired with fitted and shoes to match. Shyheed definitely has style, he thought. The choices complimented his very own style and personality. Without any hesitation, he popped the tags to a cocaine-white with red pinstripe button-down by Polo with some pitch black jeans; same designer. Scanning the line of shoe boxes, he chose the black and red Space Jam Jordan's and a Chicago Bulls fitted. A delicate spritz of his favorite "Joop" cologne and the transformation was complete. He received a fresh cut and crispy lining before being released from prison, so his appearance was all the way there. Peering into the bathroom mirror, he studied his almond shaped eyes, registering the new person staring back at him. Who was this person, this new man?

Taking his hand the length of his angular jawline, grooming his full crop beard, he was amazed at the glow and luster his bronze complexion radiated. That was that fresh home glow. Pulled from conceit, he heard the sound of Shyheed's stereo earth quaking, coming up the block. Before leaving the mirror, he told himself that he would enjoy himself tonight. No trouble. Hell, he might even find him a nice woman there. 'Yea, that would be nice', he told himself, cracking a cheesy smile.

6 SPOKEN WORDS BETWEEN STRANGERS

Bria made her way through the moderate line making admission with the low payment of two dollars and fifty cents.

"Will you be performing tonight Sistah?" the Afrocentric Sistah questioned.

"Yes. Sistah you don't mind me asking, are they friendly?" referring to the crowd.

"They can be a bit stubborn girl, but if you bring your 'A' game, you'll do just fine", she stated.

"I think I can win them over", Bria confided.

"Good. Now what will you be going by tonight Sistah?" she asked.

"Can I put 'Sexually Frustrated'?" Bria asked shielding her reply with her hand.

"Girl you'll be surprised what I hear a night. You'll be performing seventh ok? And good luck girl", she said.

"Ok, thanks."

Walking past the double doors, Bria was greeted by the mellow grove of the house jazz band. The atmosphere was luring with its dim lighting and subtle lay. The arrangement was definitely Feng shui. This gave her great comfort. Taking a booth in the rear of the main sitting area, she surveyed those in attendance tonight. The crowd was a melting pot of late teens to mid thirty-something's; business execs to street thugs. If you could think it, they probably had already thought it.

The smell of fried chicken and fries hung thick in the air, tempting patrons to pay homage to the cook. She resisted the urge to delve into her craving and decided to have a glass of Merlot instead. Signaling the waiter, he made his way over to her.

"What will it be Miss?" he questioned.

"May I have a glass of Merlot and a bag of Chicago mix popcorn please?" she responded.

"Coming right up!" he said.

Just when she thought her comfort level had reached its limit, a tall root-beer flavored Brother walked thru the door pulling the rug out from under her. Feeling the fluster of immediate attraction come over her, she fidgeted in her seat. She wrestled to maintain her composure, trying not to look like an impetuous school girl crushing over the top jock. She couldn't contain herself. Her pupils dilated and her breathing rose, the fire churned setting blaze between her thighs. Her ears, cheeks, and chest flushed red conflicting her butterscotch backdrop. Her nipples preened and her body tingled. All of this was caused by the commanding throb of love's central station signaling arousal.

"Here's your order Miss. Do enjoy", the waiter replied.

"O-thanks" she spoke softly totally oblivious to his presence.

This Brother was devilishly fine. It had to be a sin to misuse his handsomeness the way he was. He commanded attention with his 6'1", 210lb continent of rocky muscle; and he could do no wrong with his college prep meets gangster appeal. The way he rocked his low cut Caesar with perfect 360° waves and his Gerald Levert beard was ubermanly. No doubt, this Brother was premium cut certified U. S. D. A. choice cut. Looking at him standing there like an aged rib eye with all of its flavorful marble, and boy did she want a taste! Hell, she wanted the whole steak.

Taking a long sip of her wine, she further examined him with licentious appraisal. She held the wine glass in front of her face as if to hide her molesting eyes. 'How come I feel like I know you?' she spoke in her mind. 'Why Lisa couldn't have come tonight? I really could use someone to share the way I am feeling with. She was too busy getting some good lovin from this Rick guy, and when is she gone introduce me to the man who has my girl's nose wide open like the Atlantic Ocean? I sure could use some good lovin. If all goes well, it might just be tonight.' She smiled, as she closed out her subconscious thoughts.

*****

"That'll be two fifty Brotha", Sistah Madupe spoke.

"I got me and my guy", Shyheed said.

"Will either of you be performing tonight?" she quizzed.

"Yes my Queen. I will be", Tywoun charmed.

"And what is my King's godly?" she shot back.

"Tywoun at your service", he said.

"Well your majesty, you will be our eighth performer", she informed.

"Hotep Sistah", he concluded.

"Hotep Brother", she seconded.

Finding his way to where Shyheed was seated, his first impression of the arrangement was classy, and he could see they had a nice mix of serious literary scholars in the audience tonight. 'This will be an interesting night', he told himself. The performers were preparing themselves for show time. The clock was nearing midnight, and you could sense the mood had went from getting settle to performance and enjoyment. He thought the transformation was magical.

"I'm a go grab one of them chicken and fry platters. You want something?" Shyheed asked.

"See if they have some pineapple juice", he answered.

The announcer gave her formal introductory, welcoming one and all. The moment had arrived. The first performer took the stage, and appeared to be a newbie like him. Although this will be his first rodeo, Tywoun had countless hours in his mind and at prison talent shows. His only concern was getting up in front of an audience and choking on his words. He would picture the crowd in their underwear if need be, and there was some gorgeous women here tonight. Taking a look around the room, he caught a brief glance of an angelic beauty attentive to the state performer. She probably was a regular, he told himself. Not one to stare, but he couldn't help but steal a few more non-consented looks at this work of art.

"Here's your pineapple juice, and I grabbed you a few of these wings cuz you ain't getting none of mines. I'm bout to murder these bad boys, huh!" Shyheed said.

"Good lookin out my dude", he said turning to receive his food and beverage.

Insistent on catching another view of the beautifully placed unknown, he turned in his seat refocusing his scopes to be met head-on by her admiring smile. A bubbly feeling cascaded throughout him causing a childlike jitter. Returning his Kodak smile, he broke the connection before it was perceived as creepy.

The first performer left the stage while being applauded by a show of finger snaps. In the poetry world, this was the equivalent of a standard hand clap. The announcer introduced the next act then left the stage encouraging more snap. Tywoun could really get used to this type of vibe. He needed to fill his schedule with constructive accommodations. You know they say, "An Idle Mind Is a Devil's Workshop", and he vowed his resignation at the devil's workplace. Sitting there snacking on his chicken and fries, he knew he shouldn't be eating this late, or this early rather. Another mental note was made to get a membership out at the university. He had worked diligently on sculpting his hard body and would work hard on keeping it that way.

"You about up Ty, you ready?" Shyheed said sucking the crispies off the ends of the bone.

"Yea, I'm just gone freestyle one. You dig?" he asked.

"No question! Handle ya business. I always told you this was your lane my dude. Now's the time to take advantage of this golden opportunity guy", Shyheed encouraged.

"You right Brah. I was just saying to myself how I feel comfortable here."

*****

"Now, without further ado, let's give a warm welcome to our next performer. For the first time, my Sistah and yours: Ms. 'Sexually Frustrated'!" Sistah Madupe announced.

'Here we go girl, my time to shine. I've done this many times in my head before. You can do it, just stay focused', her conscience stream. Approaching the stage, Bria dug deep within the tomb of diction. Perception will portray a smooth stroke of an artist's calm hand, but this couldn't be any further from the truth. Still she composed herself with confidence masquerading as if she was a seasoned lyricist. Staring out into a multitude of eager onlookers, she took a moment to adjust the mic stand.

"How ya'll doing tonight?"

"Alright now! Take your time Sistah! Let it flow in accord," the crowd rumbled.

"Alright. Well, I came here tonight to share with you all pages of my heart, my talent from the sky, and some food for your minds. I have some things to get off my chest. So if I can borrow your ear, I'll bless them with a tune I'm sure you'd like to hear. The title of this work is called: Take Me Away. Now, I'm sure I'm not the only one in here that could use some good lovin", Bria interjected before reciting her piece......

When will you love me, to make my body scream?
To make me come alive with the music I know it will bring...
I long for your touch, your tantalizing scent,
I ask can this be permanent or a periodic event?

When will you love me, I truly need to know,
my memory is failing me – it's been so long ago.
The love I'm yearning for reaches down to my soul
making me feel jittery, like a prisoner awaiting parole.
When will you love me and give me the freedom I'm seeking?
How can you with hold from me, what I'm truly needing?
The sound of your voice, the smell of your cologne holds a spot
in my being, reminding me of home.
Baby I'm pleading, begging wanting you to love me – this is my
request, my insanity plea, when will you love me and make my body your home? I need
you to reside there, where we'll never be alone.
So again I ask, when will you love me? Please say it's soon for the passion that awaits
us will go well past the moon. My love, my heart, my soul mate, my forever tell me when
will you love me?

"Thank you for your ears tonight", she said.

And someone from the crowd shouted, "Anytime Sistah", over the loud finger snaps.

Her words spoke volumes. For Tywoun, this was an invitation too good to pass up. The words she spoke were as though she directed them in his direction. The emotion. The feel. The way she manipulated her body to match the delivery of each parable kindled the carnal flames of his detached desire. Her sincere intensity magnified appreciation, and garnered a thunderous applaud of snaps.

"You feeling her Ty?" Shyheed asked.

"Like a space suit!" Tywoun replied.

"You should go ahead and approach her", Shyheed instigated.

"I plan to do just that", Tywoun stated, as his name was announced. "That's the Ty I know", said Shyheed as he maxed a golden fry.

He took to the stage with confidence swagger, focusing strictly on his reply to her body's cry. It was a cry not of help, but the cry of compatibility and longing. He knew this all too well, and planned to minister his exact understanding.

"How's everyone doing tonight?"

"Good! Blessed!" the crowd murmured.

"How do you follow up a great performance like that? Sistah you truly piqued my interest. Now, this next piece I will freestyle, but appropriately call it, "I'll Take You There', for the lover in me, and the lover in you all. I know you can relate. Enjoy", Tywoun stated before answering her call…

☐

I'll take you there tonight
If you allow my body to act like a magnet
That draws you near;
I'll hold you tight and I'll give you
My full attention.
As I see your body structure in my mind,
All I can vision is it being my personal playground…
All you have to do is say yes,
And allow me to enter into your world tonight,
I promise to deliver good love…
I'll give you the flowers, birds and the bees.
You say you want a strong shoulder
That you can lean on;
Well here's my shoulder to lean on,
Let it be yours.
All you have to do is say:
Yes, say yes, say yes – yes is all it takes
To embark with my force of nature tonight.
You say you want to wrap yourself
Around a man so tight,
That y'all won't know where one ends,
And the other begins, well here I am…
Let's be infinite like the Energizer Bunny,
And keep going, and going, and going.
I'll take you there;
All you have to do is allow me to be the one tonight.
And we can be like the Isley Brothers
"Between The Sheets".
Where I'll display my own "12 Play" of forbidden acts
That would truly make you think
That I was under the influence.
Causing you to pull your own hair,
Like you were insane from the different sex
Positions we would explore.

And last but not least…
You don't have to worry about standing along anymore,
Fore I will be that "Erection" that keep you

Up all night long, that supports your positive thoughts,
While intellectually convincing you to disregard
Your negative one…
I know that you are afraid,
And that you "believe".
Because of the hurt you've experienced,
That love doesn't live there anymore,
But love never really vacates, it simply sleeps…
Give me an opportunity
To bring passion back into your life,
I'll make your smile so bright,
That the sun will get jealous.
In short,
Your wait is over,
Cause I'm here…
I'll take you there.

"Thank you for your time and the love you shared with me tonight, One Love", Tywoun stated before leaving the stage.

The crowd really enjoyed Tywoun, it seemed like the crowd's finger snapping wouldn't stop as someone shouted, "Talk that talk, walk that Brother…you did that Brother "T"".

*****

'Who does he think he is? With his fine self! Up there looking all dapper. Ooooh, them chestnut colored eyes, and those bow shaped full lips. Ummm…Perfection! I can almost feel the security of those big arms wrapping me in a warm embrace. And the size of his giant hands look so instructing. I wonder if he's a gentle or ruff lover. Nice and slow, or fast and steady. Who am I fooling, he can give it to me nice and slow now, and fast and steady later. I know that's right girl. I bet he's the type that'll have a Sistah beggin to go to sleep. Talking about overtime, baby boy can earn the whole check.

'No! – don't leave the stage yet handsome. I want to frame this in my mental catalogue. Where are you going love, don't leave yet. Take me with you – Ahhhhhooooo, now look what you done did, he's coming this way. What do I do? What should I say? God please don't let me mess this one up…'

"Hi, my name is Tywoun. I don't want to impede or to disrupt the flow of your evening. I was wondering if I could get to know you?" Tywoun spoke earnestly.

"So you think you can learn me in an hour?" Bria replied smoothly. "No. I believe in an hour I will know you enough to know if I can learn some more", Tywoun said with confidence.

Bria started thinking, 'You keep talking like that and I'll be all yours to know; you smooth piece of milk chocolate…' "Tywoun you can sit down if – you speak your true intent, no game, and no gimmick. Deal?" Bria offered.

Tywoun agreed, "Deal!"

"Don't you want to know my name?" Bria asked.

"You mean to tell me 'Sexually Frustrated' is not your name", Tywoun joked harmlessly.

"No silly! (Giggles!) My name is not 'Sexually Frustrated'. It's Bria and I see you have jokes."

"No. I just can't stop thinking about that smile, and the way you blush when your conscience make you feel guilty", Tywoun responded. "Guilty of what?" Bria questioned. "I'm not sure yet, but I want to know", Tywoun confided.

'Girl he wants to know you. Did you hear him? And the look in his eyes seem sincere. His presence seems so natural. I guess I'll give him a chance. Trust him girl, let 'em in.'

Over the next hour the two indulged selfishly, basking in each other's company. Sharing with one another brief history, plans for the future, personality, style, and their love of all things poetic. He gave her truth, and abated her stance of defense. He was so attentive, so interested in knowing everything that is she. This drove her wild. The way he stared far beyond her amber optics was evasive, yet handled with delicate care. Their transference of synergy was exciting and a major turn on.

'This Brother is into sorcery. The way he's spinning me in his spell', she thought. His presence was assertive, but passive when need be. Never forced, but intuitive.

"It seems our time here has come to an end. It's been a pleasure sharing it with you. Very interesting. But I'm afraid I have to be going, I have to be at work early tomorrow", Bria stated. "Give me just fifteen more minutes – I mean can you stay fifteen more minutes?" Tywoun responded.

'Girl he's practically throwing himself at you. Have you forgotten what you've come for? This is no time to back out now. It's closing time – don't blow this…'

"I tell you what – if you play nice, I'll let you come to my house. I can use the company. We can finish our conversation over a glass of wine. Deal?"

Bria invited.

"Deal! I just have to let my ride know. I'll meet you at the door", Tywoun said exceptionally.

After informing Shyheed of his last minute plans, Tywoun made his way to the door where Bria awaited his return. Shyheed was entrenched in a full blown conversation with one of the women performers, too explicit for words. A perfect gentleman, Tywoun ushered his company to her vehicle, carefully moving over the slick sheets of ice disguising itself in the pitch of the blacktop.

*****

Bria did her best to create the perfect ambience for seduction. She lit Palmaria scented candles (which was her favorite), pulled the drapes, dimmed the lights, and set the CD player on random to some mellow grooves. Tywoun stood there impressed with the layout of the house. It was a mix of elegant-classy, sexy-sassy; with a twist of sophisticated chic. He couldn't help but wonder why an educated, driven, successful, talented beauty such as her didn't have a man to make this house a home?

"You can come in and sit down. I promise I won't bite", Bria stated coyly.
"I might want you to", Tywoun replied.

"Well you just wait right here with your mannish self. I'm a go change into something more comfortable", Bria responded.

"Take your time", Tywoun quipped.

While awaiting her return, Tywoun vibed to the sounds of R. Kelly's remix to his classic "Bump n Grind". His mind journeyed back to "94" as he captured the moment he first heard this jam, and what he was doing. It was sixteen years ago at a neighborhood house party. The night he severed ties to his boyhood with the finest girl in school. Things were simpler then – he told himself. There were no worries, little responsibility, no prison record, and more importantly, his mother was here with him. He sure missed her, and her homemade peach cobbler. Those were definitely better times. Somehow he would find a way to be everything she had taught him to be; long before the streets took him away and contributed to her early passing.

"Ooooo – This my jam right here!" Bria confessed.

Snatched from his thoughts, he replied, "What you know about this?"

"Boy stop! Those were the days – twenty-five cent icy cups, cherry spurs, flaming hots 'n' Pickles, pre-sweetened Kool-Aid 'n' lemons, and afterschool dances. Things sure were a lot easier then", Bria answered.

"Yes, I was just thinking the same thing", Tywoun said.

Tywoun's mind drew a blank by the sight of her evening attire. A pair of sapphire-red boy shorts and soft cream halter top clung to the toned contours of her marvelous body. The tint of her mahogany skin shown with such luster, words only got in the way of his appreciation; so he made no attempt, he just stared.

"Can I have my body back please?" Bria teased.

"I was just admiring the art work", Tywoun confessed.

"Sure you were – you a mess, I'll be back", said Bria.

Walking away, she put a little twist in her hips, knowing he would be watching. She found it funny how natural it was to seduce an eager man. The thought brought a smile to her face, and fanned the fire generating from her core. Returning with a bottle and two wine glasses, Bria held his undivided attention with effortless technique.

"I hope you like chardonnay", she asked.

"I have a confession to make", he replied sheepishly.

"What?" she chirped.

"I don't drink. I would've said anything to continue our conversation. I'm apologizing if I've upset you", he spoke honestly.

"Don't be silly! I find it kinda cute. So tell me, what do you drink? I have soda, juice, milk, coffee, and good ole' water", she stated unphased.

"I'd like a soda please", he responded.

An hour had rolled by and the chemistry between the two had bubbled. There wasn't an area of interest that wasn't introduced into the mix. He spoke of his want to change. She spoke of the need of available good men. He went to qualities of a woman. She touched on the integrity of a trust worthy man. The two volleyed the topics back and forth like skilled tennis players. One backing off allowing the other to dominate at the net. The safe distance kept between them had vanished with every second passed. She couldn't help but wonder if he was a good kisser. With a set of lips like his, how could he not be? Wanting so much to taste his sugary goodness, she was reluctant, not wanting to be the initiator. Her old fashion standards contradicted the urge she felt to go for what she wanted.

'Girl, what are you waiting for? Kiss him! He's practically begging for it, look at him. I know, I just can't – Heifer you come all this way to chicken out now? Remember, you were going to get it off your chest, and everything will go back to normal. No strings attached. I know. I know. I think I like him though...'

It was no use, she wasn't the exhibitionist type. This was Lisa all day, not her. She wanted to be courted, needed to be understood, and must feel complete before she could share her precious gift. I guess this is why she can still count on one hand the men who met her demand. Still, there was something about him that awakened her arousal. She was very comfortable in his presence, and safe in his world. This made her resist ending the evening, but the hour was late and work called. Looking in his hypnotic eyes, she spoke, "I had a great time tonight Tywoun, and I hate for this to end. It's just I have to be at work early in the morning, and I need to get some sleep. Tomorrow will be a hectic day. I will like to continue our conversation at a later date, better time. If that's alright with you? I know you said you have yet to get a cell phone; due to your recent release. Take my number – 217-316-4321. Would you like a ride?"

"I live four blocks over. That won't be necessary. I look forward to finishing this conversation", he said, heading toward the door.

'Girl, you could at least let him hold you. It's cold out there, and you gone let him walk. That's cold. Hell, its cold in here – you can use some warm body heat. O-who am I fooling?"

"Tywoun, would you like to hold me tonight? It gets cold in here throughout the night. I would enjoy it if you would", she stated.

"I'd love to!" he answered.

"Good! I'll go get some comforters and pillows. You don't mind making a pallet, do you?" she questioned.

"I'd stand up all night if that meant I could hold you", he replied.

"Well relax and I'll be right back", she stated.

After laying the blankets down and ruffling the pillows, Bria turned to him, pulling him close. Demurely she said, "If you promise not to be nasty, I'll let you take your clothes off."

All he could do was nod his head confirming his obedience. Bria then lifted his shirt up over his head revealing a crisp white wife-beater covering his sculpted physique. Unfastening the button of his jeans, she gingerly unzipped the zipper, careful not to snag anything. Revealing a coal-black pair of boxer-briefs clinging to his tree trunk legs, she slid them down, removing them along with his shoes. Standing there, Tywoun obliged her instructions.

"Let me look at you", she ordered.

'This Brother has the body of Adonis. Um, and look at that package!'

They laid together, intertwined with her halfway on top of him. Head on his chest, she let the thump of his heartbeat carry her off into her dreamscape. She hoped that this will keep her mystery man at bay. Only time would tell.

7 DEFROSTING THE HEART

It's been days now since Lisa last talked to Rick. She was trying to wean herself from him. It seemed like the harder she tried to pull away from him, the more she wanted him. She could see his face in any picture, as well as hear his meaty voice speak to her when she was alone. The last few days have been hard to focus, thus causing her to be very irritable and moody. It didn't help that he knew exactly what to do; and say for that matter. There was the three dozen of red, white, and pink roses, awaiting for Lisa to arrive to work that Rick had sent to her job. A note was attached with the roses that read: Each rose represents the number of days we have spent together, and the number of reasons why I want to be with you. The roses came a couple of days before Rick had visited Lisa home, but was unable to get an answer at the door. He was unaware that Lisa silently viewed his painful display of inadequacy through her peep-hole. Seeing him looking the way he was brought a stage of sorry upon her, but her fear would not let her give in to his silent cries. And not to mention his voice that she could hear playing in her mind from his masterfully spoken message that he left on her answering machine. She wanted to open her front door so badly.

After Rick stepped away from her door, she replayed her answering machine again to listen to the sweet spoken words of a man that seem to be haunted by a presumptuous kind of love. A love that was worth moving mountains out of the way. A love that an ocean swim wouldn't exhaust, nor dull the intensity in its administration. She pressed the play button one more time. It played out the same as it had the fifty-something times before: "Lisa, if life is a challenge, I've found mine when I found you. It's been three days now and I guess it's supposed to be this way. Somehow, I can feel that same fear in me. Here you are in fear of being hurt, and here I am hurt by fear. I know there's questions words will never answer. So, I won't waste them here. Before I go just know that three hundred and sixty-five days, or all four seasons is not enough time for me to express why I want to live every day of my life with you, even after we stop breathing. I'll be here when you're ready. Goodbye my love."

'Why did he sound so sincere? Why is his words so convincing? Maybe, just maybe he's the one for you. You deserve to be happy too. I know, it's just I can't take being hurt. Not again.'

"Where is Bria when I need her? I can really use her company. She'll be able to help me with this situation. Yea, let me call my girl, she'll know what to do."

"Ring……Ring…….Ring……."

"Hey girl! What are you doing?" Lisa scolded.

"Uhh-oo, what's wrong?" Bria said, concerned.

"I'm bored and I'm lonely!" Lisa spat.

"I'll be there, give me a minute." Bria pacified.

"O.K., can you pick me up a fish platter from Stella Mea's?" Lisa asked, almost pleading.

"I'm on my way Hussy!" Bria said, ending the conversation.

*****

Using her personal key; Bria unlocked Lisa's front door letting herself in. The smooth melody of Sade's "Smooth Operator" foretold the reasoning behind tonight's meeting.

"Lisa!" Bria shouted.

"In the kitchen!" Lisa responded.

There, Lisa sat on her off white linoleum floor gorging on a German Chocolate Cake and a glass of Moet. Bria could sense disaster brewing just by looking at her. Lisa was confronted with a chapter she'd not read, nor was prepared to deal with the onslaught of her mixed emotions. The further she slipped, the more she indulged in the decadence of her comfort food.

"Ooo, baby what's wrong?" Bria questioned.

"Bri – I don't know what to do." Lisa stated.

"Come sit with me at the table, and you can tell me everything." Bria bartered.

At the table Bria watched as Lisa tore into Stella Mea's famous special seasoned fried perch, three cheese macaroni, collard greens, candied yams, and jumbo crab cakes.

"You want me to get you the Louisiana Red Hot Sauce?" Bria offered.

"Please." Lisa mumbled.

"Now, how about you tell me what's wrong!" Bria stated.

"Bri I believe I love him." Lisa spoke.

"Who Rick!" Bria exclaimed.

"Yes Rick Bri! Please don't pick right now." Lisa said.

"That's great Lisa. Have you told him?"

"No, I haven't spoken to him in four days. He's been calling, sent flowers – girl, he showed up on my door step looking miserable, hurt, and all I could do was look through my peep hole. I didn't even have the decency to face him and listen to his message." Lisa ran off.

"He's definitely got it bad for you. Why not give him a chance?" Bria questioned.

"You know why. I can't let him hurt me. I won't let him hurt me." Lisa answered.

"That was college Lisa. Times have changed, you're not young anymore. What are you going to do, grow old by yourself?" Bria reasoned.

"I know, I know, it just scares me to give myself in that way again, but I do believe he's the one for me." Lisa confessed.

"You know I stand behind anything you do, and I always will, but Lisa if he's that good of a man, you owe it to your heart to set it free. At least discuss it with him. Poor guy! You can hear he's hurting. Talk to him." Bri encouraged.

"I will. I knew talking to you would make me feel better and here I was getting all over you about finding someone." Lisa laughed.

"I have a confession – I think I have." Bria spoke slyly.

"Spill it Hussy!" Lisa yelled.

"Well I don't want to jinx it, but his name is Tywoun Tyrell Thomas. I met him at open mic night at the Poet's Corner. I called myself being like you, and finding something to take home. You know to check and see if the plumbing still worked. You know me, I chickened out at the last second; but I did allow him to hold me through the night. Let me tell you, I haven't slept that good in too long, and my mystery man didn't visit me that night either." Bria stated and started blushing.

"So, your mystery man formed himself finally into a physical form for you; look at it this way, no more of your wet dreams. At least the unwanted ones." Lisa teased.

"I hope you're right. He took me sledding at Berryann Park girl, you know I used to love me some sledding. It was different. Something fresh and new.

He brought his two daughters along; Brittani and Elise. We all had so much fun. Seeing him interact with his kids was beautiful. It's cute how men get all mushy with their daughter. It's like all that macho Rah-Rah gets sucked right out of them. Lisa, he even cooked for me." Bria expressed.

"What did he cook?" Lisa teased.

"We had an arugula salad with a red wine vinaigrette; sprinkled with fresh grated parmesan-reggiono. For the main course we ate roasted steaks covered in a blue cheese crust, golden brown smashed potatoes doused in olive oil and rosemary, and bourbon glazed baby carrots." Bria rambled.

"No dessert?" Lisa shot back.

"You didn't let me finish wanch!" Bria stated getting aggravated.

"Don't let me hold you up!" said Lisa as she rolled her eyes.

"So here I am grateful for this wonderful meal I had just received. When he steps through the kitchen door with a bowl of fresh whipped cream in one hand, and a bowl of mixed fruits drizzled with honey in the other. A perfect gentleman he had been all night; serving me then going back to his side of the table, but what he did next girl, made me want to eat him up." Bria elaborated.

"What did he do girl?" Lisa pried.

"He placed his chair right beside mine, still facing me. Then says, "you have very pretty lips. I ask that you let me feed them." Who am I to object, I replied, I would like that! Before you know it we had fed ourselves the entire bowl of mixed fruit and played childishly with the remaining whipped cream. I fought hard not to give myself to him that night. It wasn't easy. Especially with this sexy brother staring deep into my eyes as if he was making love to my mind. Woooo! I'm getting moist just thinking about him." Bria said, lustfully.

"And what does he look like?" Lisa questioned.

"Well, he's 6'1", 190 pounds, muscular, chocolate, low-cut Caesar with perfect waves, he has a gritty yet articulate delivery, and him and Tyson Beckford could be identical twin brothers." Bria assessed.

"I'm really happy for you Bri – you deserve a good man." Lisa said.

"If our first couple of meetings are an indication of what's to come, then I'm in good hands, but I don't want to jinx it." Bria stated.

"I have my fingers crossed." Lisa said, assuringly.

"Enough about me; how about you? Are you going to call Rick?" Bria questioned.

"I'm a sleep on it, and call him tomorrow. I guess I owe him that much." Lisa replied.

"And remember what happened in the past was not your fault. You had no control over that situation, and know you can love again. Now give me a hug and some of that cake – what is it? German Chocolate?" Bria said.

"Can't you see I'm hurting here? Why you want to eat a sister's comfort food? Here! Give me a hug, you know I love you right?" Lisa said smiling.

"I know you do, and that's why I love you back." Bria said, extending her embrace.

The mood in the room had lightened and left the two of them to indulge and enjoy the rest of the evening together as best friends. After all this is what good friends are for.

"Pour me a glass of champagne, please." Bria asked.

"Here you go." Lisa answered with a fill glass for Bria.

"I want to make a toast. Here's to breaking the shackles that bound our hearts for too long." Bria announced.

"To broken shackles!" Lisa shouted.

"Now give me some of that food." Bria ordered.

"Now you're pushing it!" Lisa spat.

"Ha, ha, ha, ha!!!" The two broke in chorus.

8 LOVE: THE SEASON IS BREWING

Tywoun stepped out this morning in an up-beat mood, with good reason. His life has found balance. He has become a positive fixture in his kids' lives, he was gainfully employed at a local steep factory; and his personal time was spent finding new ways to court his potential leading lady. Although he wondered when and if; he and Sharice would bury the ax; he was thankful they both managed to be civil for their girls' sake. It's been 3 months since he had been released, and he was proud to say he has adjusted well. He entered the toasty warmth of his newly purchased mint condition "85" Oldsmobile Cutlass automobile. Which provided him a sense of freedom, but more importantly to him was that by having his own car, he could drop his daughters off to school every morning (which was his current destination).

Today was considered a special day for him and his daughters at Washington Elementary; today was "Muffins for Dads Day." This was an event where the school shines light on the importance of father/child bonding, along with encouraging the fathers to be a vocal leader in the child's academic development. It also allows the children to display their fathers like a real life art show. Brittani and Elise were filled with such joy about today, and their dad was just as excited as they were. All he could think about is how he never had the pleasure to attend any of the past events, and he refused to let anything keep him from making it with his kids today. On his way to get his daughters, all he could think about was his childhood, and he made a vow to himself to not let his kids go through the turmoil he had with his father. None of the broken promises, missed birthdays, or holidays. His goal is to make sure they had all they could imagine, but mostly he would devote as much time as needed to ensure they didn't head down the wrong path as he did the first half of his life.

"Honk! Honk!" the horn announced as Tywoun alerted the girls of his presence. Without a moments break, Brittani and Elise burst out the front door full of laughter. Only stopping to briefly wave good bye to their mother.

"Bye Momma!" Brittani sang. "Yea, Momma Bye! See you after school." Elise shouted.

"Bye –bye babies, make sure you two behave yourselves." Sharice responded.

Out of good gesture, Tywoun extended a friendly wave in Sharice's direction. Returning his wave in a show of respect; she flashed a cordial grin of appreciation. Turning his attention back on the girls; he made sure Brittani was fastened in properly, and helped Elise strap herself in the back seat.

"How's Daddy's baby girls doing this morning?" He asked, issuing good morning kisses.

"Fine!" Brittani replied. "Daddy you get to meet my teacher today." Elise said.

"She's not going to tell me you've been bad is she?" He teased.

"No silly! Well, there is this girl named Laya that be getting on my nerves Dad, and we be arguing and stuff." Elise said, truthfully.

"There's this boy in my class named Corey, and last time we had Muffins For Dads he was being mean saying we don't have a father and that's why our mom had to come." Brittani reported.

"Don't worry about what Corey said okay, because your Dad is here, and I will be at every Muffins for Dads from on out baby." He said dauntingly.

With that said, the three of them made their way to the school; where a day full of events awaited. Arriving, the scene was chaotic and full of spontaneous combustible children. Their echoes roared through the halls. Their giggles rumbled through the rafters. The little busy bodies weaved in and out of traffic; fathers in tow. Their destinations were unknown and each one had so many stories to tell. The fruity smells of fresh baked sweet breads tickled the noses of the anticipating taste buds, stirring hunger. The fathers in attendance took great pride in being there; Tywoun felt the same. For him this was his obligation, his duty, a responsibility he would not allow another to fulfill again.

"Mrs. J! Mrs. J! Come meet my Dad." Brittani said, excitedly. "Good morning Brittani, and how are you Elise?" Mrs. J greeted. "I'm fine Mrs. J, this my daddy!" Elise boasted. "How are you doing Mrs...?" Tywoun paused. "Mrs. Ja'Angela. All the children find it easier to call me Mrs. J." She spoke, extending her hand.

"Forgive me, Mr. Thomas." He stated, shaking her hand.

"Yes, Mr. Thomas – I've heard so much about you. Please excuse me we're about to get started. I need to make some final adjustments, but please see me when this is over so we can discuss these two promising stars. Don't worry girls I have nothing but good things to say about you two." She said, with a wink of the eye.

After being seated the program started and the speakers gave their dissertations. An hour had passed leaving the kids antsy and seeking their fathers' attention. Putting a wrap on the gathering, those in attendance were released to the cafeteria to enjoy strawberry, blueberry and banana nut muffins along with warm cups of hot chocolate. Tywoun relished in the moment and the looks on the kids' faces. This was definitely an event to remember, and he made a note for the date of the kid's next school event. Before leaving, Tywoun stopped in on Mrs. J. as she requested. Leaving the girls to run and play with schoolmates; he and Mrs. J. went over some gray areas bringing color to this murky situation. He was delighted to know that his girls were a smart pair that didn't need much instruction. Mrs. J. also told him that they flourished in many areas, and focused on building up the others. Brittani showed great compassion in helping fellow classmates, and she was always encouraging. Elise was bright and bubbly with an extreme love for basketball. They showed a close bond with one another, and were very respectful to others. Well, aside from Ms. Elise's snappy remarks nothing was amiss. As Mrs. J. smiled, she also warranted that Elise actions were just a part of her unique personality, and it was perfectly fine. Never critical, only insightful Mrs. J. encouraged and promoted Tywoun's hand on approach.

"So many parents, fathers in particular pay little or no attention to the academic achievements in their children's lives. Together we must promote literacy, functional math skills along with one, or two special skill traits that will allow them to excel later on in their lives. I commend you Mr. Thomas for the father you are, and the father you will be. It's not always ease, but it sure is worth it when you see your child become a responsible adult conducting their lives by the morals and principles you helped instill in them. It sure is an irreplaceable feeling. You have two beautiful little girls that will go far in life, you just make sure you're around to witness it." Mrs. J. said.

"I will be here, and thank you for your time today. I will be active along with their mother in the advancement of their lives. Again I thank you for your time. Thank you!" He replied.

"Anytime Mr. Thomas, take care, and have a nice evening." She stated, extending a handshake.

"And likewise." Tywoun quipped, excepting the gesture.

*****

Bria sat at her desk this morning sippin' on a hot cup of green tea. Snuggling deep within the grooves of her favored chair; she hummed to Usher's "You Got It Bad," as the steam from her tea played curiously across her frozen face. The weather conditions outdoors was a typical day for the region. But not even the weather could erase the fetching smile that was displayed on her face. She sat in a moment of bliss; felling fortunate that she too could experience what others unselfishly bragged about. Since meeting Tywoun her life after work consisted of more than a glass of wind and journal entries. Just this morning before she left for work, Tywoun showed up only to shovel away the freshly fallen snow, so Bria would have a clear path to her car. His selfless act only made her more appreciative of him. It showed he was kind, considerate, and caring. Which in return was worthy of a little; oh, who was she to be stingy – a LOT of brownie points. His act led to an invitation for a dinner date, her place, tonight, to repay for his deed.

The commotion in the office fell on her deaf ears as she vamped with the subjective realm of contentment. She asked herself what exactly she was looking for. She wanted to be loved, and needed to be understood. The love must be reciprocated. 50/50 no exceptions! Was it too much to ask for an incorrigible love full of solidarity? Caught up in her thoughts; Bria was oblivious to the adamant call of her name.

"Bria! Bria! Bria!" her co-worker shouted as she leaned over her cubicle. "Bria!"

"Huh? Awe Janet, what's up girl?" Bria said, disengaged.

"Damn Bria are you okay? I called you like four times. Anyway, a few of the girls and I are going to step out this evening, you want to go? We'll probably stop by the Starlight for Happy Hour, then head over to open mic night at the Poet's Corner. You down?" Janet asked.

"I appreciate the offer, but I have plans tonight. Can I take a rain check?" Bria replied.

"Come on girl, it's been forever and a day since we all got together and had some fun. You're the only person I know that would rather sit around the house, doing God knows what, instead of enjoying yourself with your friends. You really should get out more." Janet said.

"It's not that I don't want to step out with the girls; it's just that I have a dinner date tonight. So don't be trying to make me feel guilty." Bria responded.

"So that's why you are over here glowing in a daze. So, who is he and what's he like?" Janet questioned.

"Well, let's just say; Tall, dark and handsome." Bria stated with a big smile.

"What! No more?" Janet shot back.

"I'll keep you posted." Bria replied.

"You do that, and by the way, I'm happy for you Bria. Call me and let me know how it went." Janet concluded.

"Okay" Bria stated.

"This work day needs to end," Bria thought. All she could foresee was getting home so she could start preparing dinner for Tywoun tonight.

*****

After leaving work that evening, Bria stopped by the County Market to pick up a few what-not's for tonight's extravaganza. Once she got the items she needed and paid for them, she wasted no time in getting home, so she could start preparing her evening meal. Pulling into her driveway she truly appreciated the maintenance of her walk way Tywoun had cleared. She was glad that she didn't have to trudge across the arctic floor sloshing around not knowing where the slush ends and the ground begins. She smiled with delight as she exited her car and made her way into the house. It was truly wonderful not having to stomp off her feet, or to clear the ring of cold wet snow that always seem to find itself around her freezing ankles. What a blessing that was. She placed the groceries on the kitchen counter before going to change into something more comfortable. She decided that her soft pink sweat suit and her matching Nike Air Max would work just fine. There was a spine grabbing draft splintering throughout the house; which was due to the old Victorian structure which the house was designed and built. Setting the thermostat to seventy-five degrees, she listened as the heat came alive. As she started to warm up, she turned on the radio to listen to some ol' dustys. The mellow voice of Kenneth "Babyface" Edmonds serenaded her with his masterfully versed, "I Give Good Love." "That's my jam!" She spoke to herself while organizing the various items she had purchased from the grocery store on the countertop.

Tywoun was due to arrive in the next half hour. There was something about his presence that made her anxious as if it's their first time meeting, every time. She had never experienced this feeling before with any other man. He was different, unafraid to be himself, self-sufficient, very creative, genuine, and a great father to his two beautiful little girls. That alone would have any woman swooning over a man. The bubbly feeling that comes over her just at the mentioning of his name was much like grandeur. This hold, this life sized infatuation was very much real and understandably appealing. How can one resist that which didn't exist? This gravitational pull towards longing, love, life and laughter was welcomed.

Tonight will make their twelfth formal assemblage. And other than the night they first met; the night he held her in his sheltered grasp, he hadn't made any attempt at sharing her warmth. Although his craving was apparent in the way he looked deep into her hazel eyes. He remained a gentleman allowing her to be the executor of her estate. This was another one of the many reasons why her body called for him in the still of night. Mentally she wasn't sure if she was ready, yet physically there was no question her body yearned for his qualified touch. Images fornicated within the walls of her mind; causing a stain of gratified embarrassment to saturate the base of her satin laces panties.

"Cool it now Girl! Don't you go thinking for both of us." It was better this way. A man enjoys a good chase; the pursuit of the hunt. They are dominating creatures. If awards are giving without achievement; they will move on to their next conquest unfulfilled yet satisfied. To tame the beast you must with-hold treats. This was something she swore by. It wasn't a matter of will she; it was more a matter of when. It had to be when her brain shut down, and her heart deviated the orders. Conscious of her importance; she would conduct herself by the very standards and values her parents had instilled in her. Nothing else!

There was a light tap at the door. "It must be him," she thought to herself. Checking the time she wasn't surprised to see he was early as usual. This told her he valued the time set and shared between the two of them. "There's nothing wrong with extras." She spoke out loud. Glancing out of the peep-hole; she took an "extra" moment for an uncontested survey of his stylish handsomeness.

"Look at you with your fine self." Bria greeted as she open the front door.

"From where I stand you're the only beauty I see." Tywoun spoke cool and collected.

"Come in here out of the cold silly." Bria said, grabbing him by the hands pulling him inside.

Tywoun consented himself to her parental will, and was greeted with a pleasant hug and peck on his left cheek. The hug was more love interest then "hey, how you been, nice to see you again." Taken back by her sudden display of affection, he wondered what had gotten into her. Since the night he held her body so close to his very own; there hadn't been any contact between them, friendly or otherwise. Well, there was the night they fed one another strawberries 'n' whip cream with their bare fingers, but this was a different kind of contact. This contact was provoking and condescending. Marveling the view from the back; he held her a few seconds longer appraising the meaty hump protruding from her powder pink sweatpants. One can only imagine what it was like for him, fresh off an eight year prison sentence, sexually deprived, and hungry for release. The animal inside of him wanted desperately to come out and play, he promised he'd play nice.

After hanging his leather jacket on the coat rack, he was led to the kitchen. Where tonight the two of them will play chef, host and hostess.

"My, my, what do we have here?" He asked.

"I thought it would be nice if the two of us prepared our meal together. Seeing that you have the same passion for cooking as I do, I thought we'd share the kitchen. You know, teach each other a thing or two." She replied with the cutest smile.

"I would like that." He told her returning the smile.

"Good! We can get started. I hope you like lasagna topped with ground beef, pan seared pancetta, bell peppers, onions, sun dried tomatoes, and mascarpone and buffalo milk mozzarella cheese. Then we'll toast sweet French loaf in the broiler with garlic and butter. On the side will have a light baby spinach salad tossed in a honey Dijon vinaigrette. Afterwards if you have room left maybe I'll give you something sweet. So you better eat all your vegetables!" She said, playfully.

"Yes ma'am, for you, I'll eat 'em all. No lie!" He quipped obediently.

"That a boy." She replied.

Together they were a tag team duo; tandem of sorts. She set the water, as he diced the vegetables. When she would instruct; he would follow. Step by step the two moved on one accord all the while enjoying each other's verbosity. For him this was as interesting as when the sun fades across the melting sky leaving a collage of selected beauty in its wake. Remarkable; never has he felt so lively! There were nights when he would lay in his rack; looking up at the various cut outs of gorgeous women taped to the bottom of the top bunk, and envision all of the significant things he for too long took for granted. Never again! Not in a million years would he trade in nights of love curious passion, for the demoralizing days of prison reformatory. When he was with her he was free. Free to fly, free to dream, free to be absolutely free. It totally helped that her bubbly personality and her infectious smile was warmer than the awakening of a midsummer sunrise. For this, he was gracious.

Bria was amazed at how easy it was for the two of them to work together. This knowing how men can sometimes be stubborn and un-excepting of a woman's guidance, and the unappealing way women can be self-centered in their approach. It brought a big smile to her face as the thought crossed her mind. This was definitely another check in the "pros' column. The team work displayed was an influential indicator that she had found someone who meet her 50% of the way. Not just in preparing a meal, but dealing with life in general. This was a rare find, a precious gem. One she had hoped to relish in its antiquity for many years to come.

"Just take it slow girl, it's only been a couple of dates, and you're already thinking years down the line. I don't want to burst your bubble, but right now what you may be seeing is his representative. I'm just saying, take your time; that's all."

"I know, I know." Bria spoke out loud.

"You know what baby?" Tywoun questioned to her unwarranted outburst.

"Oh- I was just saying I know I can't wait until the lasagna is done. I'm hungry, how about you?" She stated inconspicuously.

"I'm definitely ready to eat. I haven't eaten anything but a muffin all day." He replied.

"A muffin!" She responded as if shocked.

"Yea, today was "Muffins for Dads Day" at the girls' school." He spoke in excitement.

"Awe, that's so cute how you glow when you talk about your kids. By the way, how are they doing?" She asked.

"They're doing really good in school. I'm just happy that I've been allowed to be a part of their lives, I mean the three of us have become really close." He answered.

"That's great you are a good father. I'm happy for you all." She said.

"Ding!!!"

"Lasagna done!" Bria quipped.

Bria had taken the time to prepare the dining room for a romantic evening. The mood was magnified by the fluttering flames of the jasmine scented candles playing childishly in the backdrop. There was no music just the sound of conversation and laughter. The perfect gentleman; Tywoun went to plate the dishes, but Bria would have none of it.

"Tonight is your night, just sit back and enjoy." Bria said patting his hand away.

Comforted by the notion that she was catering to him; he cracked a welcoming smile as she placed a hearty slice of cheesy lasagna onto his plate; followed by a piece of buttery sweet French bread and salad. Since Tywoun didn't drink alcohol, Bria chose Hawaiian Punch instead. While enjoying their meals they discussed life and various subjects of interest. Bria shared her love for life, and depicted an enchanting tale of her happily ever after. She wanted nothing over the top, just sustainable success, and an abundant amount of tranquility, a good man with considerate intentions, and a matrimonial tie to forever. She also went on to express a deep seeded desire to one day (when the time is right) welcome the nurturing presence of motherhood.

This all boded well with Tywoun as he went on to share what he calls, "Love, Life and Opportunity." These were three aspects he believed if understood would bring optimal balance to his existence. He then went further explaining one must first love self in order to live a healthy life. Then and only then can one capitalize on the opportunity to distribute this very love unselfishly. Tywoun's eyes lingered in the maple brown lenses of Bria's attentive eyes emphasizing his sentiment. There was much to share, and over the rest of dinner the two dove deeper into an intriguing pool of revealing conversation.

"May I ask you a question?" Tywoun asked.

"Sure!" Bria answered.

"Do you believe love can set a person free?" Tywoun questioned.

"Yes, but only if a person is willing to remove the shackles around their heart." Bria answered.

Over the next hour, both Tywoun and Bria gained a new sense of understanding due to the unbridled trust they felt for one another. After they finished eating dinner and cleaned the dishes, Bria grabbed a pint of vanilla ice cream and the fresh fruit tart she'd purchased earlier from her favorite bakery. Then she led Tywoun into the living room where they fed each other the sweet treats over light conversation. Bria wanted so much to kiss his alluring lips! His lips were a delectable distraction from the way they glistened with the milky rich residue coating them, or by the way they wrapped around the spoon with their velvety softness. Bria imagined his lips searching her canvas for her archeology find. An archeology that had been fossilized for quite some time now. Bria's body suddenly reached a degree of white heat. A reaction that was brought on by her lustful longing to be handled, Bria couldn't help but cross her legs in hopes of calming the perpetual throb coursing through her privacy. The more she resisted, the more she ached.

Her inner goddess wanted badly to enjoy if not forever, at least for one passion filled night with this god. Her body cried "FREE ME!", yet her heart feigned caution.

Oh – who was she kidding, Bria had all but given her heart to this man, at least verbally anyway. She placed the pint of ice cream between her thighs praying that it would cool off her fire. To no avail, the vibration from Tywoun getting another spoonful of ice cream reverberated throughout her body crying, a crippling spasm causing an unwilling release.

"Mmmm!" escaped her lips.

"That good huh?" Tywoun asked feeding her the spoonful of ice cream.

"Oh, you have no idea." Bria answered.

Tywoun enjoyed the art of seduction, it was something he paid careful attention to. Seduction is paying attention to detail with subtlety. Almost as if to control the subconscious. This is what he set out to do from the first bite of ice cream they shared.

"Do it girl, just do it, kiss him…I want to, I do; it's just I can't…Now's not the time Bri, don't do this to us…I know, I know, but I wasn't raised that way, I guess I'm just old fashioned."

"I had a really good time tonight Tywoun." Bria stated.

"You know, with you must be what it's like to be complete because I find when I'm alone I wish you were there with me." Tywoun responded.

"Awe! That's very sweet of you. I have a secret. I think of you constantly too." Bria confessed.

"I'm honored to know I cross your mind." Tywoun stated.

"As much as I wish this night didn't have to end, I must start preparing myself for work tomorrow." Bria said reluctantly.

"Yeah, I need to be getting home." Tywoun agreed.

"We have to do this again if that's alright with you?" Bria extending an invitation.

"I would love to. How about this weekend? That's if you don't mind the girls coming along, I will have them this weekend." Tywoun relayed.

"That would be fantastic. I think that's a great idea, they are so much fun." Bria answered.

"How does Sunday sound?" Tywoun asked.

"Sunday will be great." Bria replied.

"Good, then it's a date." Tywoun said.

Tywoun motioned for the door as he stood making an attempt to pick up the empty carton of ice cream and tart tray. Once again Bria reminded him that this was his night to enjoy, not work. Courtesy was fortunate to know such a man. He flashed a smile placing the garbage back on the table. Bria placed her feminine hand into his massive mit, and guided him to the coat rack. The way her hand fit into his, made her feel secure and safe from any harm. Why was it again she had sworn off men, beside the fact that most men are shallow, selfish and systematically taught to be dogs? Oh – and there's work to blame. Whatever the answer, she was far from caring. All she knew was she felt a natural progression of coupling between them, and it didn't hurt that he could set blaze to her desire like no man, myth or legend for that matter. The time had come and it almost hurt to let go. This is what scared her more than anything. Never again she confessed that she would open up to that kind of pain, but somehow she actually trusted that this man would do her no wrong.

"Bria I must say that being here with you is like the stroke of an artist's hand, every stroke of his brush leads him to his master-piece. I just want to say that my picture won't be complete until you're in it. Again, I thank you for tonight, and goodnight." Tywoun spoke.

"I believe in your picture Tywoun, good night, and drive safe going home," Bria said, giving him a hug and light kiss on his cheek.

Bria's body tingled with sensation as she laid her head against his defined chest listening to his heartbeat. Why wasn't his heart beating like hers was? Bria trembled beneath his touch asking herself is he capable of causing this reaction within her forever? God she'd hoped so! The next moment took her totally by surprise when Tywoun took her chin in his hand bringing her to eye level. Just then he kissed her softly on her ready-to-receive lips. Fireworks went off inside of her as joy filled her heart, and the obvious in her already sodden panties. Bria had long craved his taste wanting to identify with his flavor. Tasting his ingredient Bria lost herself giving back what he had started. The two held each other as they satisfied the thirst that long since purged the backs of their throats. It was at this very moment time stood still.

"You go girl! Find your release…No! Wait!!! What am I doing?"

"No…Please…Stop…I shouldn't be doing this." Bria said, pulling away.

"I'm sure you have your reasons." Tywoun stated releasing a great sigh.

"It's not you…I mean…I want you; it's just," Bria tried explaining.

"Baby I understand, I do." Tywoun answered.

"You do?" Bria asked.

"When and where will be your choice. Besides, I've not shared myself with anyone in eight years, six months now. I can wait for when the time is right." Tywoun replied.

"I'm sorry Tywoun; I really am." Bria apologized.

"There's no need Queen. Get some rest and have a good day at work tomorrow. I'll call you tomorrow evening." Tywoun spoke soothingly.

"Okay, goodnight." Bria stated turning to open the door.

Bria's insides cringed with regret on one hand; while on the other she felt that she'd done right. Still she was disappointed more so for her concern with his need than her own. Back pressed up against the front door; Bria found the energy to make her way to the bathroom. Where she would take a hot shower then go to bed.

9 ADMITTING TO LOVE

"I hope when you get this message you find it in your heart to forgive me. I know I have been very distant. I'm scared, but I believe I owe it to you, to let you know why. Call me when you get this message okay; bye-bye." Lisa spoke into the receiver.

Hanging up the phone, all she could do was hope Rick would call her back. The knots in her stomach sent a river of nausea exciting fits of discomfort. Her hand clammed up as a light sheen of country apple scented perspiration formed along the detail of her shaken frame. She thought she would never have to relive that night. The thoughts were horrible. Being ripped abruptly from a lifetime of unfulfilled promises, endless recreations of every dream she had dreamed of, and the love that life's cruelty had taken for her. After several years of therapy, the nightmares stopped and allowed her to pick up the pieces of her life. Repaired yet fragile she reinvented herself; becoming the self-assured, independent socialite many knew her to be. What started as a precautionary measure turned into a way of life. That's until Rick came and penetrated the leather tough scar tissue apprehending passage to her susceptible heart. Her fear turned to joy by the feeling he brought upon her; she just hoped it didn't ruin her.

Hours passed finding her hopelessly at the bottom of a pungent blend of fermented grapes. Her pride kept her from crying, but the guilt held her accountable. Sitting by the phone she felt foolish; on top of being alone. What could she do, or what could she say? After all, it was her selfishness that pushed him away. The irony cut like a serrated knife leaving her exposed to blunder. Still, it hurt to let go. Sunken by a torpedo of failure she was submerged in a sea of bitter disappointment. Blotting the corners of her tear stained eyes she whispered; "I will not cry, I will not cry, I will not cry." It was to no avail because the tears flowed like raging currents. Sprawled along the floor in a fetal position; she held herself trying to keep from shattering. She managed to pull herself out of this drunken stupor. "Maybe a hot bubble bath will make me feel better." She said, consolingly.

The soothing effects of mint julep wrapped her in a maternal warmth. With her knees pulled tightly at her chest she rested her head upon them, and wept. Her soul was hurting, and regret was the reason why it condemned her without good interest. Wanting to be held she compensated by manipulating the bubbles to form an affectionate caress. Smooth was this touch. Eyes closed she created a place in time where his love was king. He held her so gently, so soft, as he took her sensuously into the heavens. Physically his prowess was strong; but tender when needed to be. A jack of all trades; he reached miles in one single bound. The way he loved her in this very spot was electrifying. Caught in the stimulation of this memorable moment, she wished she could somehow transfer this feeling elementally. How she needed his touch; his intoxicating kisses, the way he brought omneity to her life. These were nothing but fond memories, because here she sat all alone focusing on the incoming ring of his much anticipated call.

After washing away the pain she moisturized then curled up on the sofa with a box of assorted chocolates. Even this made her think of Rick. She would pick through the box nibbling each chocolate to see which where her favorites, discarding the ones she didn't want to him. These moments were of bittersweet taste. She thought about calling Bria, but decided that she wouldn't bother her with her problems, she would handle her situation herself. Just her and the lifetime channel. The portrayal of a love sick woman was contrary in likeness. After a while her eyes grew heavy drawing sleep near with every yawn. Clutching the cord phone to her breast; she thought to herself, "just in case."

Looking up at the clock mounted over the mantel; the hour reached early in the morning. Rising from her slumber she conjured her equilibrium before taking to her feet. As she rubbed the soreness at the base of her neck; she turned the television off. She walked to the kitchen to get a glass of milk to cut through the dryness that was in her throat. Once she finished the glass of milk, she made her way to the bathroom to relieve herself. Before getting in her bed, she made one more stop, her closet where she retrieved one of Rick's "Polo" shirts. Which still had his scent of Johnson & Johnson's Baby Magic Lotion and "Body" by John Paul Gaultier which he liked to wear. She then climbed in her bed holding and sniffing the shirt she had with her. After laying in her bed for a while, she flirted with the idea of some self-gratification. Her body craved to be touched, and was possessed with a salacious lust. Oh- how she wanted to be handled by her man, her Rick. The earth stopped spinning he came to perform, and he always showed appreciation by ending his performance with a standing "O."

She clenched her thighs tight trying to subdue her aching throb. It was no use, the force was too strong. Not wanting to seem desperate she reached for the phone, and dialed his number. After a few rings the other line was answered – "Hello". Rick spoke groggily.

"I…really need you right now Rick. I know I've insensitive and I promise I will explain, but baby my body is calling, calling for you to come make love to me. Can you hear her? She's calling your name baby. We'll be here waiting, and Rick…I love you." Lisa said before hanging up the phone…

Desperate times called for desperate measures, and this was no time for subtlety. She was very aware of the power of the p-u-s-s-y, and had no qualms pulling out the big guns. After all, they could talk afterwards. Right now it was about curing her body from the burning fever it had, and Rick was the only one who had the medicine to cure her illness. There was no way she would go without him, it just wasn't fathomable.

Setting the tone; she lit a couple of Midnight Passion incense, and cued R. Kelly's classic twelve play album to, "Your Body Calling." In the mirror, she applied "Juicy" lip gloss, and sprayed Strawberries 'n' Champagne body spray in all of her intimate areas. Deciding at the last minute to go with her hair down; she positioned the full curls to hang seductively onto her face. One more last minute adjustment and she would be ready for the taking. In nothing but his Polo shirt, she sat at the edge of her bed listening for any signs of his arrival. The reflection of headlights from an oncoming car ricocheted off her window pane dancing in the darkness. Like an unabashed schoolgirl, she flocked to the window giddy with excitement; it was him. Her heart fluttered as her legs trembled beneath her. Without hesitation she ran to the door to meet her Boo. With synchronized succession the two greeted each other in unison. Pulling him out of the cold and back into her life, Rick was shocked by her eagerness.

"Take me to the top baby and keep me there until my love comes down." She spoke, lustfully.

Rick being such a willing lover wasted no time in locking his lips to her; his kissing immediately sent shock-waves throughout her body. With his masculine arms he swept her up off of the floor carrying her straight for the bedroom. Passion burned bright in both of their eyes. Once they reached the bedroom, together they stripped him of his clothes. Without saying a word, she laid back on the bed spreading her legs to allow him to enter her throbbing body. After sliding into her, he started swimming through her silky sky. His thrust was ferocious. Her glide was slick and slow. Her emphatic cries sung lullabies of genuine pleasure, as he pillaged and plumaged in search of her hidden treasure. Sailing the high seas of desire he rocked back and forth in her crashing waves. Brought to the brink of explosion, somehow his seed was saved. Excitement never felt this tangible. Love never tasted so sweet. To him, she tasted like cherry jelly beans. To her, he was a Hershey treat.

"Deeper baby, deeper!" She cried out for his love.

Exodus took form transferring them into a gamut; out there beyond sanity instinct promulgated perpetual bliss. Intertwined standing still is what's left of time. He set the rhythm, and she conveyed the rhythm. Closure tickled deep with his stomach, and tingled up and down her spine.

"Cum with me baby!" She sang, lost in translation.

As night playfully awakened a new day; he tilled her soil and fertilized her field. Leaving their joy overflowing, spilling chromosomes free to roam in the valley of life. Laying there tangled in each other's arms secure and safe from any harm. Not once or twice, but three times was her charm...

"Rick, baby, I want to share something with you. Something I believe you deserve to know. I really trust you, and my heart tells me that I'm right. There's really not an easy way to tell you, but here goes.

Back during my freshman year of college, I was engaged at that time to the love of my life. His name was Mateen Mitchell. We met each other our junior year in high school at Hannibal High, twenty miles up the road in Hannibal, Missouri. We were your typical seventeen year old couple, too many hopes; so many dreams. He was your All-American Athlete and I was class valedictorian with an impressive 4.5 GPA. I opted to attend Quincy University to be closer to home so I could help my mother with my father's failing health. Mateen received a full athletic scholarship to play basketball for Michigan State University where he planned to follow in the footsteps of "Magic" Johnson, his favorite player.

During a summer pick-up game right before he was to leave for school; he suffered a career ending injury to his right hip. After surgery rehabilitation was hard and grueling. The doctors told him he had sustained the exact same injury that ended Bo Jackson's career. Mateen was stubborn, and felt he could overcome his injury and live out his dreams of becoming the NBA

Finals M.V.P. It was hard watching him put himself through the long fruitless hours of torcher. It was no use, and to add insult to his injury everyone turned their backs on him. What a culture shock! It was like we woke up and nothing in life was the same. Time passed and we tried to pick up the pieces. He decided to join me at Quincy University so we both moved to Quincy. That's when he proposed. It was like, "finally things were back to normal." There were talks of obtaining our doctorates, starting our own business, and having a few babies; thus, live out a happy ever after life.

One night we were coming home after a couple of parties and a few drinks, well, maybe too many drinks. Somehow or another, I'm not certain, but an argument was stirred up. He wasn't the man I was set to marry that summer in our dream wedding. He was mean and said some very hurtful things. Things he wouldn't say if he wasn't tipsy; I'm certain of that, it wasn't in his character to say the things that he said that night. Hurt by what he said, I lashed out at him. The passing of words led to a full blown argument; I said some things; he said some things. Before we made it home, our engagement was called off, and my heart was broken. With our future in limbo and the alcohol fueling our bull-headedness, Mateen dropped me off at our house, and stated he was going for a ride and he'll be back later. Wanting the night to just end, I didn't question it, nor did I think to care. I, I can still see the look in his eyes today. I didn't mean what I said, I was hurt; so I responded callously. I would do anything to take my words back that night. The next morning after I awakened from a fitful sleep, I noticed he wasn't in the bed with me. I thought no big thing, he's probably asleep on the couch. So, I walked to the living room to see if he was indeed on the couch, but he wasn't there, nor was he in the house period. I tried to call his cell, but there was no answer. I was like "wow!" could he really be that upset about our argument last night, it was just built up frustration. Probably due to school, work and the wedding coming up in three months; the pressure had gotten the best of us. I was sure we would kiss and make up after we got over our fallout.

Anyway, I fixed myself some breakfast and got ready for school, it was getting close for my first class to begin, so I left out headed to school. I tried to stay focused, but I was worried to death.

Around ten that morning on my way to another class, I received a call from his mother on my cell; thinking she was going to ask what went on last night between Mateen and I, I braced myself. Nothing could have prepared me for the news I was about to receive. My heart was snatched out when she told me he was in a bad accident, and he didn't make it. My world had ended and guilt threatened my sanity. After years of therapy, I've managed to pick up the pieces of my empty life. I made it through that situation, but I vowed that I would keep my heart locked away safe from any more pain. That is until I met you. Honestly, I never saw it coming. Nothing had prepared me for you. You came and rekindled the light that long since had dimmed. Baby, I fell for you hopelessly, yet I fought it. Not because you weren't life's companion, rather, if I had accepted the opportunity to learn your love I must strip away my armor, so that you may learn mine in return. So please understand Rick that I was not pushing you away. Being here like this, vulnerable and open for everything that love brings; I would be naïve not to take into account that with love comes pain. All I ask is that you make your love for me pain free, and continue to do what it is you do, because when you do it, baby – you do it so right. "Can you do this baby?" She asked.

"Lisa, I'm sorry for your loss, and I want you to know your strength that's seen you through that situation and to see you here now, strong and unbroken is very admirable. It shows character and resiliency. If life was never meant for us to be as one, then Lisa I will spend the rest of my life with no one. So, to answer your question, these hands of mine are gently enough to hold your heart. Trust me. Let my love set you free", he replied pulling her body close to his.

"Promise?" she murmured.

"Cross my heart and hope to die" he told her.

"Stick a needle in your eye?" she teased.

"Promise!" he assured her.

Elation would best describe the mood between the two of them. Over the next two days they locked themselves away for the weekend, and copulated time and time again spoiling one another with their love.

10 LOVE ON THE HORIZON

There was an implausible calm at the work place today; a calm that Bria accepted with open arms. The last thing she needed after a long night of unrest was to come to work and be bombarded by the usual office antics. Surprisingly, there was order over the floor as she stepped off the elevator and made her way to her cubicle. Bria removed her coat hanging it on the back of her chair as she logged into her computer. In need of a jolt, she decided to get a cup of hot java to help boost her work day.

"Yea, that'll do the trick." She whispered under her breath.

Pouring a hot cup of the premium blend, Bria was joined at the coffee maker by Janet and Pam.

"Hey Bri, so how did it go last night?" Asked Janet.

"Good morning girls, it went well." Bria answered.

"It sounds like you could use some sleep", Pam stated with a smile.

"I didn't get much last night." Replied Bria.

"That good huh?" Janet insinuated.

"No wench, I didn't give him none." Bria spat.

Deep down Bria wished she had given Tywoun some, hell; all of her wouldn't have been enough. All night long she had fought back the urge to call him up, and have him to come and unlock her love. Damn! This man was good. Bria tried her hardest to focus on work, and not as much on the mundane thoughts in her mind. Being as though it was Saturday, Bria knew she needed to complete the final draft for her column, also proof read the entire Monday issue of the '411' weekly. A few stimulating sips of her caffeinated beverage and Bria found her groove as she escaped into a world of informative expression. Eight hours and three cups later, Bria had finished her weekly column, and proof read all but a quarter of the entire issue. She decided it would suit her best to finish up at home after a nice hot bath and a satisfying meal. Gathering her things, Bria shut down her computer, stopped for a brief moment to talk with Janet and tell Pam good bye before leaving the office.

*****

Once Bria arrived at home, she called her main girl Lisa to invite her over for dinner; so, they could talk about the latest adventures that may have occurred in their lives since they last spoke to one another. Which happened to be when Bria went to Lisa's house to rescue her. Bria was wondering if Lisa had called this Rick character. After the fourth ring Lisa's voice mail picked up. Leaving a message Bria hung up and went to prepare her bath water as she undressed waiting for the tub to fill. After she had finished bathing, she dried off and slid into a comfortable pair of jeans, hoody and some air force one tennis shoes. She checked her phone to see if she had any missed calls. To her delight there was a text message from Lisa.

It read… "I'm in love can't talk right now. I'll call you when I can. LOL…"

This explained why Bria hadn't heard from Lisa in the past two days. A smile warmed the corners of her lips. Bria was truly happy for her friend. She knew it took strength for Lisa to set free her heart. For too long Lisa locked away her feelings, and turned a deaf ear to loves call.

"I'm proud of her." Bria spoke to no one in particular.

Bria would have to enjoy her meal alone this time. No problem. She decided to fix herself a grilled tuna melt on whole wheat toast, along with a side of avocado fries. After preparing her meal, she poured herself a glass of pomegranate juice and dug in while finishing up the editing of next week's issue. Afterwards, she planned to curl up in front of the cozy fire, and doodle today's entry in her journal.

Dear Journal,

Today I managed to think of no one but him. I know, I know. This entry starts just as the last one did, I mean, it's just – "God!" this man seems to have some kind of hold over me. Why is it that I can't think of anything other than his warm chestnut eyes, golden bronze skin, mmmmm……and those lips…yes, why is it I can't think past his lips? The way he kisses me is so playful, yet so inviting. I don't think I've ever felt this strongly for any man before. I ask myself what is it about this man that makes me feel this way. He's kind, and for that, I'm grateful. He's courteous and for that I can't complain. He seems to

be genuinely into me. Oh, and the way he interacts with his girls is more than encouraging…., by the way, I think he is so sexy, and for that, I have no shame.
 Bria…

*****

Why now after all this time of living alone did Bria find herself lonely in her own home? Staring down at her wrist watch it seemed as though the time refused to carry on. Having completed her work and not wanting to watch reruns of Girlfriends; she decided to call it a night, even though it was only a few strokes past 8pm. She thought to call Tywoun just to hear his voice, but decided against it. Tonight, Tywoun had his children, and she felt she would be selfish to impede on their time. She sure could use his conversation, the way he gave her his undivided attention, and yes his heat. It hurt to think of the pleasure he was sure to bring, because of an unwavering bond with morale. The dictation of standard presumably withheld Bria from unbridled release without commitment. Old fashioned or just plain sick and tired of the emotional letdown; Bria preferred the latter.

After flopping around like a fish out of water, Bria laid in her bed entangled in the covers. Sleep didn't come easy, perhaps it wouldn't come at all. This display of childish agitation only poked fun at the absurdity of her current state. Would she continue to ignore that in which refused to be shut out any longer? The question played continually with her conscience.

"I'll just call to say goodnight." Bria reasoned with herself.

Moments seemed to turn into an eternity as Bria waited anxiously for her distant lover to receive her call. On the third ring just as she was going to hang up, he answered.

"Hey love, I was just thinking of you."

"Oh, you were, were you?"

"Yes. I had just put the girls to bed, and I was wondering if you too were thinking the same?"

"And what's that?" Bria replied.

"That you just had to hear my voice."

"And if I was, you promise not to let it go to your head?" Bria responded with a smile on her face.

"No, I won't baby, only a big heart."

"Okay, yes I was thinking about you."

The two shared a brief laugh.

"Tywoun, I want to do something special for you." Bria said with a serious tone.

"And what do I owe for the honor?"

"I feel terrible about last night, so I want to make it up to you."

"And what do you have in mind?" he replied with a deep since of interest.

"I want to make love to you." Not believing what she just said, she covered her mouth with her hand.

Silence left a void as Tywoun registered the sentiment in Bria's words. The earth's axis must have tilted more towards the sun, because there was a warmth reverberating through his core far hotter than this gaseous star could ever burn. Could it be the time had come, here, right now? His loins hungered to feast greedily on this delectably preserved meat. How his tongue wanted to know such a flavor. His hands craved to handle the smooth tapestry of her honey suckled skin. Just the mere thought of burying his face in the heaven of her neck; which irresistibly reeked of strawberries 'n' champagne incited his inner animal to run wild.

"Tywoun, did you hear me?" Bria asked.

"Yes, for a minute I was at a loss for words. Are you sure you're ready?"

"Not yet physically, but mentally I'm ready to learn you Baby."

Not exactly what he was expecting, Tywoun considerately allowed himself to play her game.

"You lead and I'll follow." He suggested, smiling from ear to ear.

"Mmm...It's been a long day, and all I've thought about all day long was coming home to you. Now that I'm here, I want to do something I'm sure you'll enjoy!"

"And what will that be?" Tywoun asked.

"What is it you ask?" Bria shot back.

"Do tell." Tywoun said, as he grinned.

"Well, since you've been so good to me, I want to convey my appreciation for all that you do. Please allow me to relieve you of these clothes, you won't need them on this journey."

"Journey!?" Tywoun asked curiously.

"Shhhh, don't talk for now. Just listen as I guide you over my wondrous land, thru my pristine valley, and enjoy as I take you for a dip in the rejuvenating currents of my sun warmed stream. Now, please sit and watch as I dance for you, but first Honey would you be so kind as to press play on the C.D. player? Ssss...I feel so hot right now Baby, and it's because of you."

"There U Go," by Johnny Gill is playing softly in the background. "It's as if I'm a slave to the beat. I can't control myself. It's you that I want, it's you that I need. I stare deep into your eyes, and I see you're anxious. I am too, but I promise you the wait will be worth it. Trust me. I speak love's language, and your eyes speak the language I love. View my body I'm here for your viewing pleasure. As I dance for you I start to feel the folds of my honey hole slicken with gratified temptation. My scent grows louder and louder the more I whine my hips to the music. I don't know what has come over me, but I like it. Do you like it Baby?" Bria asked.

"No question! Don't stop!" Tywoun stated.

"Well come over here and dance with me. Wrap me in your persuasive embrace. Oohh…your flesh feels so good pressed up against mine. Touch me Boo don't be afraid my body's yours to do as you like. Here, give me your hands. Do you feel that? That's fire flowing thru my veins. At this moment I feel so alive, so aroused. You cup my face gently in your strong hands as you lean in to kiss me tenderly, you're sweet like coconut's milk. You steal my breath away with your mystical powers. No…Baby don't stop I want more, please just one more. I love how you make me feel. I then place two warm kisses in the palms of your work worn hands. Watch as I guide you down the slender slopes of my neck, up around the baby soft skin of my shoulders. Go ahead Ba, playfully kiss me on the collar bone. Mmm…that feels good…right there. Advancing to my free roaming breast. That feels wonderful. My nipples ache to be sucked on. Can you accommodate me kind sir? Hmm…Hmm…that tickles…Ooooh yes…right there. You know you'll spoil a woman with skills like yours. Don't forget the other one. While you dine, I rub the pattern of waves in your low-cut Caesar. My stomach muscles flinch when you caress the small of my back. We continue to dance close, and I feel your manhood throb between your legs. You want me, don't you?" In a sexy voice Bria asked.

"You know I do." Tywoun answered with excitement.

"I won't make you wait much longer, promise! I'll take your male member and stroke gently from the base to its plum shape tip slowly. I see you tremble beneath my touch. Which excites me. Can you imagine how it's going to feel inside me?"

"Soft as silk Baby." Tywoun replied.

"Why don't we see, palm my ass and lead me to the bed. Now lay back on the bed – what was that; you want to taste me?"

"uhhhuhn!"

Taking my hand deep inside my sticky bowl of confection; I stir my finger in its sugary syrup before pulling my hand up toward your eager mouth. "Taste me…You like?" Bria whispered.

"Uhhhuhn!" give me more, Tywoun replied.

"There will be time for that later, now I just want to feel you inside me. Next I straddle you while I place you safely within me. Sss…It feels like a thousand feathers are working me all over. Blood rushes to my nether region as I work figure eights over your sculpted frame. Climax is near. Baby, you fit me well. As I rub over the area of your well defined abs I kiss a trail of wet kisses leading to your neck. Hmm…you smell great. What is it?"

"Gucci, by Gucci Sport."

"It smells so good on you, it's a turn on itself. Rub my back Ba, and help guide me. Waves swell as my ocean rolls. Anchored deep there is no way the coming storm would wash you away. The way you grope and knead me, all of my tense spots are so relaxed. Oooh, Tywoun my love's about to come down…Oooo cum with me baby. Give it to me…Mmm…Sss…Here it comes…Oooo I'mmm…Don't stop, don't stop!!! I'm cum-in…yes, yes, yes. Thank you Tywoun for allowing me the pleasure, and thanks for being so understanding, you just don't know how much that means to me. Once again, thank you and have sweet dreams…Goodnight Baby!"

"Sweet dreams Baby, I'll see you tomorrow."

After hanging up, Bria shuttered under the power of an intense orgasm. Satisfied for now, she retrieved a wet wipe from the night stand cleaning up the residue of contentment from between her legs just before she fell asleep.

11 LOVING ON AN IMPULSE (OR NOT)

"Rick what am I going to do with you? It's been two days since we've come up for air." Lisa said, lifting her head from his chest.

"Yes, well, my love has no limit; besides you're running around here naked in all of your sexiness making it hard for a brother to leave." Rick spoke with poignant swagger.

"You got your nerve!" Lisa shot back as she raised the satin sheet viewing her well-oiled machine.

For the previous two days, the two fornicating lovers had survived off of nothing much other than a carnal banquet which was the consummating force of their survival. No work. No communication with the outside world. Just the both of them, every room in the house, and the various positions they fed their love. Could this last forever? The feeling of an incredible sense of wholeness. Lisa, although apprehensive at first was left defenseless when confronted by an all too familiar feeling of serendipity.

With her heart warmed to the idea of dancing with fate; Lisa beamed with delight. Not quite sure on what would be waiting for her when she got there, but she was prepared to embrace the unexpected. It was now, or never, and who was she to turn down the ordained intermissions of what's supposed to be? After all, this chiseled piece of onyx lying next to her was more than a blessing. More like a gift from the gods. At least, Lisa felt that way.

"Rick what are we going to do?" Lisa asked as her head lay across his chest while she listened to his heartbeat.

"Why don't we get away for a while? I don't know, maybe see the world." Rick stated.

"Are you serious?"! Lisa answered sitting up with lightning speed.

"Yea, why not?"! I've always wanted to see the Fiji Islands." Rick replied.

"Oooh…Brazil, Spain, China!" Lisa ran off with child-like innocence.

"Just say the word." Rick insisted.

"Ooo…but what about work? We can't just pick up and leave." Lisa cried out in agitation.

"Relax we can take an early vacation."

"Yes, why didn't I think of that – I have to tell Bri!" Lisa said, excitedly jumping out of bed.

"Good! While you do that, I'll contact my travel agent." Rick hollered down the hall after her.

12 MY NEED TO KNOW YOU

"Girls, remember I need you two, to be on your best behavior tonight okay?" Tywoun said, to his daughters with his back turned as he pulled the roast from the oven.

"Daddy you really like Bria don't you?" Brittani questioned.

"She's a special woman Brit." He answered.

"More special than Mom, Daddy?" Elise cut in.

"Your Mom is very special Honey-Bun, it's just unfortunate that time and distance grew us apart, but your Mother will always be special. One day you'll understand kiddo." Tywoun said, playfully nudging Elise on the chin.

"Oh, Daddy not you too; Mom says the same thing!" Elise shouted dramatically pounding her palm against her forehead in a show of sarcasm.

"Yea Dad, we don't have to be adults to understand not everything works out the way we want them too." Brittani rebuked her father's statement.

The girls helped arrange the dinner table while preoccupied in sibling banter. Tywoun looked on proudly as the two jostled one another back and forth with adolescent paraphrases. The lingo of today's youth has evolved far passed the razzing of his day. Still, many memories of his childhood were ever present in the interactions of his daughters. For a moment Tywoun couldn't believe he was free and about to share a home cooked meal; prepared by his own two hands with those that truly mean the world to him. Moments such as these substantiate his reasoning for changing his life's type.

"Daddy the door!" Brittani yelled in excitement.

"It's her Daddy come on!" Elise shouted gleefully running towards the front door.

"Coming, coming." Tywoun stated falling in stride with the girls.

"Open it, open it Daddy its cold out there, hurry!" Brittani said, impatiently.

Inside Tywoun felt overwhelmed by the rush of emotion surging throughout him, Bria certainly had a firm hold on his heart.

"Hi Bria! Hi Bria!" Brittani and Elisa both greeted her enthusiastically grabbing both of her hands dragging her inside out of the cold.

"Hi, you two, I brought you something, I hope you like it." Bria said, cheerfully.

"Easy girls, easy!" Tywoun said, trying to conceal his own excitement.

"Oh Daddy, you know you're just as happy!" Elisa said, respectfully.

"Yea Bria! Dad thinks you're special."

Brittani revealed shamelessly.

"Oh, he does, does he?" Bria responded giving Tywoun an appreciative eye smiling.

"He says you're very special." Elisa egged on.

"Okay, I'm busted, you got me. Now allow me to help you with your coat and those bags." Tywoun said, jovially.

After hanging Bria's coat and relieving her of the two gift bags, Tywoun and the girls led Bria through the house to the kitchen where the pleasant aroma of a well prepared meal awaited. Bourbon glazed pot roast, with pan sauce fingerling potatoes cooked in rosemary, sea salt, olive oil and fresh cut asparagus was a dinner sure to please. Seated, Tywoun did the honors of slicing the mouth-watering roast, giving everyone a hearty piece along with sides.

"Mmm…Daddy this is really good." Brittani said.

"Uuhnhuhn!" Elise shook her head in agreeance.

"The girls are right, it is delicious Tywoun: Bria fell in chorus.

"I can't think of three more deserving women, thank you." Tywoun said graciously.

Conversation was splendid over the reminder of the meal. The girls pulled Bria a hundred different ways with their inquisitive prodding of what she had hidden in the gift bags. It was no use, Bria withheld the remnants in the bags with unwavering resolve. Still kids will be kids, and they tried their hardest to get Bria to spill the beans. Tywoun sat back and viewed the girls' interactions with Bria. It was comforting to know that if things between Bria and him were to get serious; which he believed would happen, it's a must that her and his daughters obtain a great relationship among the three of them. He refused to be like so many other parents who just disregard their child's opinion of their new mate, due to blind love, or better yet their own selfishness. Tywoun knew and understood that his children had to be the integral factor in the remainder of his life while he was on this earth. Even after leaving this earth, he planned on watching over them from the sky. So to see this natural bonding process take form (especially between three special women) right before his eyes only encourage his already deem able heart more toward Bria's gravitational heart melting commitment. It was there, in that moment Tywoun convinced himself that Bria was all he ever wanted in a woman. There was nothing more he needed to know, sign his love on the dotted line.

Tickled with laughter Bria looked up catching Tywoun's gaze with admirable adoration. Their eyes seemingly spoke the words their mouths were not yet ready to speak. It was evident in the others lingering glare the battle was won. Love most certainly was the victor. The two shared a warm smile as though they were taunting the spoils of war.

"Daddy can we play Candy Land now, can we?" Elise pleaded tearing the two adults from their dreamscape.

"Yea Daddy can we?" Brittani seconded.

"That sounds like fun." Bria instigated.

"Why don't you ladies go and set up while I clean up here, I'll be just a sec." Tywoun stated.

"Girls why don't you two go and setup. I'm going to help your Dad okay?' Bria spoke stacking the plates.

"Okay" the girls shouted as they scampered off...

Finally the enraptured couple stole a moment away from the kids were they could display their uncensored show of affection.

"You know, I'm still high off last night." Tywoun stated placing his hands around Bria's statuesque hips pulling her close.

"I don't know what got into me last night." Bria replied trying to conceal the stain of embarrassment shading her smooth café au lait complexion.

"You look beautiful tonight Bria." Tywoun comforted lifting her face from the safe burrow of his chest.

"You truly are a wonderful man, and great father." Bria said, finding the courage to look into the sincere pools of his hypnotic eyes.

"Share with me your life Bria. Be my Queen, my equal, the only woman I go to sleep and wake up next to in the morning." Tywoun said, adamantly.

"Are you serious?" Bria questioned hesitantly.

"The girls can't get enough of you, I'm falling in love with you, I crave you throughout my day, and I breathe in your scent which makes me afraid to exhale because I'm scared that I might never get it back, yes I'm serious; serious as a heart attack. Love me Bria, and I'll unconditionally love you in return." Tywoun exclaimed.

"I can't stand another heart break Tywoun, please be gently with my heart." Bria responded with tears not of pain, but those of happiness in her eyes.

"Kiss me love." Bria order.

Their lips locked capturing time storing it away for safe harbor.

"Oooooh!" Brittani and Elise teased with their little heads peeking around the corner.

"What am I going to do with those two?" Tywoun said, cracking a toothful grin.

"Come on Ba, let's go play Candy Land, and let the two little angels see what's in their gift bags." Bria replied leading Tywoun into the living room; where they enjoyed the rest of the evening laughing, playing and creating the first of many memories to come.

13 BLINDED BY THE MYSTERY OF LOVE

"Oh Rick, the water here is so clear; it's beautiful. I love it!" Lisa spoke passionately as she viewed the rich teals, turquoises, and the unseen blues for the first time.

"Yes, but not as beautiful as you." Rick spoke lovingly assisting Lisa down the steps of the plane.

"Welcome to Wakaya Club and Spa, Mr. and Mrs. Moss. I will be your guide, Kemo. Please come with me, I will show you to your villa." The warm natured assistant greeted the couple.

Kemo tended to his duties loading the luggage into the back of the awaiting Land Cruiser. Lisa and Rick filled the back seat soaking in the scenery. Nothing would've prepared the two for the exquisite beauty, no mind could conceive. The lush terrain was covered in emerald forest, white sand beaches, gravity defying cliffs, sapphire tinted lagoons, and a collage of unharmed coral reefs. The view was amplified by the sights and sounds of the exotic wildlife carrying on haphazardly without a care.

"It's just up the road here, we'll be there shortly." Kemo stated over his shoulder keeping his eyes fixed on the road.

"Honey, I'm so excited!" Lisa replied resting up against Rick.

"I'm glad you like it." Rick responded.

The soft tropical air mixed soothingly with the salt laced breeze that drifted up from the sea, and the floral decadence of the frangipani. Birds of some sort flew curiously overhead as if to say: Welcome.

"We're here!" Kemo announced their arrival.

There it stood, Wakaya Club and Spa in all of its splendor. Surprisingly, the resort wasn't overtly commercial. Made of bamboo, coral, braided coconut husk fibers, and locally cut wood contrived the beautiful landscape that sits at a northwest angle facing the charismatic lee shore. Ten bungalows in all, the retreat felt pleasantly expansive. In the foreground the Koru Sea thrashed back and forth making its might presence known, spouting mists of indigo in the air, then setting back into its massive burrow.

Nineteenth-century lithographs and maps draped the woven walls, which were made of palmetto, in the reception area. A bounty of books were shelved on the bookshelves. Artisan rugs covered the wood flooring.

"Please, Mr. and Mrs. Moss relax; you are among friends. My name is Windell, I'm the activities coordinator. There's much to do, but let's get you two settled in. Program itineraries are posted on the walls in every bungalow. Forgive me, where's my manners! May I offer a taste of paradise? Your throats must be parched." Windell ran off in repetitive sequence.

"Yes, thank you." Rick conceded.

"Mmm, this is so delicious!" Lisa paid her thanks in compliments.

"Yes, well enjoy, because that will be the last time you will taste that certain blend my Queen. The locals hand pick and blend these wonderful concoctions differently each time, but no worries, the next one is always better than the last." Windell said, gleefully turning to escort them to their honeycomb hide out.

"I can get used to this!" Lisa stated sipping her drink.

"Say no more, I plan to do just that." Rick answered reassuringly.

Stepping out into the breath taking ambience of what could easily be perceived as heaven on earth. Rick slid his free hand in Lisa's hand following Windell blissfully with Kemo and luggage in tow. The mid-day sky shone bright Carolina blue fused with the richest shade of royal enigma, while the gently winds stirred the alabaster clouds in an imaginary bowl of ecstasy. The view was miraculous to say the least, birds soared to unforeseen heights, blossoms were in full bloom, and the florescent creepy crawlers scurried atop the blades of the manicured lawns.

Arriving at the bungalow which was named after a native tree: Evuevu. Lisa knew at first glance lavish comfort was just on the other side of the veranda.

"Your chamber awaits you with luxurious amenities to accommodate your relaxation and leisure pleasures. I guarantee seven days and six nights will not be enough, trust me, I've been going on fifteen years now. Unpack, unwind, freshen up, I'll have your noon meal sent over. Do either of you have allergies?" Windell expelled courteously.

"No." The couple answered synonymously.

"Good! I have just the thing. Oh, before I go; there will be one more couple joining us this evening, but don't worry the grounds were built for ultimate privacy. Just in case the two of you might want to share your company. Kemo, let's leave these vibrant love birds to their lover's quarrel. Kemo, or myself can be reached by radio for anything. If not, it will just be you and the lovely Queen"

"Rick." Rick stated, accepting Windell's extended hand.

"Rick, ah yes, and you Madame?" Windell finally went over the formal introductions.

"Lisa." Lisa stated as she crumbled under his regal charm.

"Now that we are acquainted; I'll be off – just so you know, the stars hang like iridescent light bulbs in the night sky. Love is better made with that view." Windell said, with such brashness.

"Oh my!" Lisa replied in shock. I'll be sure to keep that in mind, thanks." Rick stated, seeing the two men to the door.

Rick turned surveying the spacious sitting room appraising its sophisticated chic décor. It had an upper Manhattan feel with a Laguna Beach undertone. It put Rick in the mind frame of crisp linen slacks, flip-flops. For him this was a match made in heaven. Rick took a sip of his drink before following the rummaging sounds coming from the bedroom. Lisa was weaving in, out, and around the bedroom immersed in a string of "Oh-My-God!" chants. There, in the middle of the floor sat a four-poster king bed, draped in the finest Italian linens, accented with a plethora of fluffy throw pillows.

"Wow! Honey come here and check this out." Lisa shouted from the bathroom.

Turning away from the bathroom, Lisa looked out of the bedroom's double paned glass door were she noticed an airy outdoor shower fenced in by a wall covered with the black volcanic rocks. As the sun soaked sky served as the ceiling for the shower. Lisa stepped outside to get a closer view of just what else was on the other side of double-paned glass door followed by Rick.

"Oooo, I can't wait to make love to you Baby, out here." Lisa stated to Rick.

"Why don't we start christening the premises now?" Rick proposed.

"You must have been reading my mind…" Lisa replied unlacing her soft cotton sun dress causing it to fall from her body onto the floor.

Rick immediately unbuttoned his shorts, causing them to drop to his ankles as he pulled his shirt over his head, throwing it to the ground. Walking toward Lisa, he scooped her up in his arms, only to carry her back inside to the bed, so he could enact the animal that was within him.

Placing here down on the bed as if he was putting a child to rest; their eyes focused studiously on each other. Rick slowly started to kiss and lick on Lisa's curvaceous body, starting from her head, going down to her toes, and then making his way back up; stopping at her honeycomb as she moaned softly as he kissed and licked between her inner thighs.

Lisa placed her hands on Rick's head gently caressing it as she continued to moan which sounded like a love ballad to his ears. The sounds of pleasure coming from Lisa's mouth were causing Rick to become very excited. Causing him to invade her honeycomb with his stiff tongue; which instantly caused her body to quiver.

Within minutes, her body started to shake from heavy convulsions caused by the special techniques of Rick's stiff tongue.

Rick knew he was about to accomplish part of his mission. As Lisa arched her back, removing her hands from his head only to start hitting the bed with the sides of her fist. Suddenly, Lisa started speaking in a voice as if she had caught a Sunday Morning "Holy Spirit" at church...Ooo- Ooo baby – Ri – Ri – Ri – Ooo – Rick – Ric – Baby - Ba – Ba – Yes – Yess – Ooo – Ooo – Right There – Mmm – Don't stop Ba – Baby! Were the last words she said, before her body became stiff; she made one more twist as she braced herself just before releasing the honey that was within her honeycomb. Within seconds Rick's face was covered with Lisa's precious honey, which he joyfully captured every drop that presented itself.

After completing his intake of Lisa's honey; she told him to bring his candy stick to her as she opened her mouth. Rick did as requested, and Lisa immediately started sliding her mouth up and down his candy stick; while twirling her tongue around it, causing Rick's toes to curl...Reminding him that he wasn't the only person in the room with special tongue techniques.

Sensing that he was becoming very excited, she released his candy stick from her mouth. Arranging herself into a doggy style position, she invited Rick to invade her honeycomb once again.

He quickly lined his manhood up, and slowly slid into her honeycomb, grabbing the side of her hips to pull himself deeper into her wet and warm honey nest.

The friction caused by the constant moving of back and forth, and grinding from Rick, caused Lisa to release a great amount of honey from her honeycomb.

After unlashing a large amount of honey; she knew Rick was about to release his manhood. She looked over her shoulder and told him to replace his candy stick into her treasure box; and once he got in, to relief himself.

Once again he did as he was asked, to his surprise, he had no problem gliding into her treasure box due to the amount of honey that was stuck to his candy stick. The special grip that he received after his entry was just too much for him to handle. He could no longer keep from exploding, he leant across Lisa's back and wrapped his arms around her stomach tight. The time had come, Rick relieved himself like a high power rocket headed into orbit. Lisa looked back toward Rick and asked him did he enjoy; he softly said, yes as if he was out of breath. Lisa wiggled her body, smiled and said, wait for the next round.

14 FALLING HARD

Tywoun ended another shift at the steel plant, he wanted nothing more than to be able to soak his exhausted body in a steamy hot shower. Tonight he had planned to enjoy a little rest and relaxation since Shanice and the twins were having girls' night, and Bria had to work late due to a project she was working on. As Tywoun gathered his belongs before clocking out and heading toward the front door, he thought about what he could do to occupy his time.

"Mr. Thomas, may I have a word with you in my office?" his crew foreman asked.

"Sure", Tywoun responded, stepping into his office.

"Please have a seat – I've been doing some thinking, and I've come to the conclusion that you would be the best man for the job.

"Job!?" Tywoun replied puzzled.

"Yes, how does shift supervisor sound?" the crew foreman asked.

"That sounds great Mr. Gordon." Tywoun replied with joy.

"Please call me James. The hours are long, and the work is demanding. There's also a significant pay raise that comes with the new job as well."

"When can I start?" Tywoun questioned.

"Stop by my office when you get in tomorrow morning, and we'll go over everything. Now go home and get some rest." James ended their conversation.

"Thank you!" Tywoun stated as he turned to leave.

Tywoun was all smiles on his ride home. Excitement filled every muscle fiber in his body, making it hard to focus on the road. He turned on the radio in hopes he'd distract the rampant thoughts that was racing through his mind. It was "Mad Issues Monday," on the Michael Baisden Show. An unhappy audience member was putting her no good baby's father on blast. Tywoun thought just six months ago he too was also considered to be a dead beat dad. He couldn't fathom how a man could deliberately neglect his own flesh and blood; anyone for that matter.

Tywoun decided to ride through his old neighborhood to kill some time before heading home. He saw Shyheed and a few other locals he knew were standing out on the corner enjoying the recent weather change. Springtime was slowly emerging with the hotter days of summer approaching, which brought out many spectators to enjoy the much anticipated break from the choke-hold of winter.

"Ty what's hood?" Shyheed greeted him with a pound.

"On my way in, I just stopped to holler at you." Tywoun replied.

"What's on the mind?" Shyheed questioned.

'I – ', "Shyheed cut'em off." Let's step over here. I know this ain't your crowd anymore, you being a working man now. Na – for real though, I'm proud of you Ty – now go ahead, what were you about to say?"

"I just got a promotion." Tywoun stated, trying to conceal his excitement.

"That's what's up! Now you can do some of the things you talked about – like moving Shanice and my nieces out of the projects." Shyheed stated.

"Off top I want to do that. It's just convincing Shanice to swallow her pride, and work with me on this." Tywoun said, showing concern.

"I guess now's a better time than any, here comes Shanice with the little ones now." Shyheed said, motioning with his eyes.

Turning toward the direction Shyheed had signal with his eyes, Tywoun spotted his family coming down the block.

"Daddy! Daddy!" his daughters shouted as they ran toward him.

Arms stretched wide Tywoun scooped them both in a big bear hug, and placed kisses all over their faces.

"Daddy, Daddy, I thought we weren't going to see you today cuz it's girls night?" Brittani asked happily.

"I know Honey Bun, I just stopped to talk to Uncle Shyheed." He answered.

"Hey Uncle Shyheed!" Brittani said.

"Yea, hey Uncle Shyheed!" Elisa seconded.

"Hey little ones," Shyheed replied.

"Daddy, Mommy's taking us to the park. You wanna come?" Brittani asked.

"I thought it was just us girls today?" Shanice stated in general.

"A Ty, I'm let yall talk, hit me up later, we'll celebrate." Shyheed said, walking off.

"Celebrate what Daddy?" Elisa asked nosily.

"Yea, Dad." Brittani seconded.

"Daddy got a promotion at work today." Tywoun revealed.

"That's great Dad!" Brittani responded.

"Daddy what's a promotion?" Elisa asked.

"It's when your boss believes you deserve more responsibility, and more pay Sweetie." He answered.

"Aw, that mean you can buy us more toys huhn?" Elisa quipped.

"Hush, child!" Shanice scolded… "We better get going before the sun goes down. Girls, tell your Father bye."

"Bye Daddy!" the two said, somberly.

"Bye!" Tywoun couldn't understand why it was so hard for Shanice and him to communicate. After all he's assumed his position as a full-time father, and has done all he can. He told himself he wouldn't let this ruin his day. Still he'd wait patiently for Shanice to let bygones be bygones.

*****

Bria was dreading working late tonight. There was so much she'd rather be doing, like enjoying a memorable wrapped within the warmth of an affectionate night sky, a glass or two of wine, and her new man. Yes, this would be wonderful. The only problem standing between her thoughts and reality was – she had taken on the responsibility to revamp the company's magazine. Which required her to donate her nights until she was able to come up with a new and improved look for the magazine. She was torn between obligation, and the newly emerged wanting to be in the presence of love. She wondered what Tywoun was doing? Probably with the kids, or at the gym working on his perfect picture body. "I wish he'd call." She thought better yet, "I'll just call him." She reasoned.

"You guys continue working, I'm going to use the restroom." She told her colleges.

She entered the bathroom stall locking the door behind her. Why she didn't know. She guessed it made her feel safer. Retrieving her phone, she was surprised to see that Tywoun had sent two text messages. Reading them, the first one stated how much he missed her; which made her smile. The second message was telling her about his new job promotion, which made her very proud for him.

Hitting speed dial on her phone, she listened to the music on his ring back.

"Hello, you're now speaking to the new supervisor of Knaphied." Tywoun answered.

"Baby I'm so happy for you. That's wonderful!" Bria replied happily.

"Yea, I'm still trying to come to grips with it myself." Tywoun responded.

"I'm sorry I can't be there to celebrate with you."

"No big deal Baby."

"I promise to make it up to you this weekend."

"That sounds great. I'll probably step out with Shyheed for a couple games of pool, then I'll call it a night.

"Enjoy yourself, and call me when you get in, and by the way I miss you too." Bria said, before she said be good and bye.

*****

Half sleep, Bria looked up at her alarm clock wondering who could be knocking at her door this time of night. Gathering her senses she made her way to the door.

"Who is it?" Bria asked.

"It's me!"

"Tywoun."

Opening the door Bria was shocked to see Tywoun standing there battered and bruised.

"Oh my god! Tywoun what happened to you?"

"Can I come in?" he asked.

"Sure, let me help you."

Bria led him into the kitchen and told him to sit down in one of the chairs at the table. She turned on the warm water in the kitchen sink and told him "I'll be right back, I'm going to get somethings to fix you up."

She returned quickly with a first-aid kit in one hand, and peroxide and triple antibiotic ointment in the other. She tended to his wounds with a nurse's care. Tywoun winced from the pain as she applied the bandages.

"There, all better and done. Now please tell me what happened." Bria said with great concern.

"At the pool hall some guys started causing problems and being rude, I wasn't looking for trouble, I was just trying to keep everything at peace. Out of nowhere this guy swung on me. So, of course we started fighting, while fighting I noticed that Shyheed was also fighting with another guy. The next thing I know, a female comes out of nowhere and hit me across the head with not one, but two bottles while saying leave my man along." What....

"Hmm...Hmm...nothing Ba, I'm sorry; it's just that you look so cute and innocent, almost like a child explaining what happened. I'm sorry, go ahead."

"When the police arrived the fight was over, the bartender told them what had happened, and she informed them that Shyheed and I only defended ourselves. So, I don't have to worry about my probation officer...Thank

God." Tywoun said.

"And you came here cause you wanted your woman to take care of you?" Bria said, smiling.

"Yes, and because I missed you."

"Well come on let's get you cleaned up."

In the bathroom Bria turned the shower on for him.

"You want me to help you with those?" Bria asked, speaking of his clothing.

"Be my guest." Tywoun said, with a grin.

Stripping away each layer of his clothing, all Bria could do was gawk at the sight before her. In her eyes he was perfect. Right height, good looking, well defined, and "God!" the brother was packing. Looking at the symmetry of his tree-trunk like legs, she thought of the positions he was surely capable of executing with pistons like those. A warmth rushed over her, and it wasn't due to the suffocating steam snaking its way from the shower.

"You like?" Tywoun asked, Bria.

"You're simply delicious." Bria responded.

"Join me." Tywoun said, inviting Bria into the shower with him.

"Oh, I wouldn't miss this for the world." Bria replied with a super smile.

Their hands touched playfully as they stared lustfully in each other's eyes. It's been a long time coming for Bria, and for Tywoun it felt even longer. Bria truly wanted to be in this moment, this place of timeless exploration; it almost hurt the feeling was so strong. "Kiss me." Bria breathed barely above a whisper. Obediently he complied with her command. His hands molested the confines of her slickened frame; not in a sick pedophile way, but in such a way stirring the sticky nectar that had begun to drip from her core. The aroma chemically charge his arousal awakening a hunger deep within his loins.

"Wash me, and I'll do the same for you..." He stated, as his eyes fornicated over her firm yet submissive body. They lathered one another, spending more time over the more intimate areas inciting uncontrollable ohh's and aah's. Before long, neither of them could resist the other's cry for a climax. Rinsing, it was evident the time had come, and there was nothing going to stop this measure from unfolding here, and now. Together they exited the shower, once dry this love scene transferred over into the bedroom. The cool draft brought life to her delicate nipples. Robust and full of life her fleshy nubs ached to be fondled, and sucked. Letting the damp bath towel drop carelessly to the floor; she carried out a few necessary adjustments, lightning candles, and some "Eternal Love" scented incense.

To her delight there he sat at the edge of the bed massaging the healthy portion of meat dangling between his spread legs. All she knew was she wanted him, but for now she had to have him in her mouth. As she approached him the butterflies in her stomach subsided bringing forth a confidence that was new and ferocious. Sexy was her stride; almost feline like, "Purrrrr…." She moaned on all fours as she crawled the remaining feet between them. She then placed a velvety trail of kisses up his leg until she reached her destination." Here, I'll handle it from here." The feel of his most sacred of flesh in her virgin hand was smooth to the touch. She buried her nose at the base of his manhood, inhaling deeply, so she could register his scent. Exhaling, in a sigh of relief, she then applied the perfect amount of tongue feeling him shudder under her power. Which only help boost her confidence. With the grace of a ballerina, and the know-with-all of a bona fide freak, she performed pirouettes up and along his lengthy shaft. Taking him deep into her mouth, slowly she bobbed up and down swallowing on reflex granted him deeper access.

Bria was so turned on by now, her inner thighs were coated in her secret ingredient. Standing she spoke, "Love me with no boundaries…I'm yours, but first taste me…" Tywoun jumped quick to her request, repaying with his mouth what was owed to her. Skillfully he gave her orgasm after orgasm with his many oral tricks.

"Lay back…" she shivered coming down out of the stratosphere.

She took her place atop of his majesty, inserting his royal scepter safely in her silk woven womb of pleasure. Around and around she took him on a carousel ride of joyful wonders. Never too little, and always as much as he could handle. The rhythm of his husky grunt blended with the mellow moans of her brilliant octave recorded the soundtrack to their duet. She loved the way he filled her to capacity, quenching her thirst, and satisfying her appetite. The feeling brought tears to her eyes. Never before had she given herself in this matter, or fashion. With him she felt special, like the rarest of diamond been given on an anniversary, or even as the breath of a child; so full of life. Perhaps he was heaven sent, or better yet, crafted specifically to her likings. One thing she was sure of, she was madly in love with this man.

Tywoun's world was spinning; it had been almost ten long droughtful years since he'd enjoyed the carnal call of physical gratification. This was new to him, love before sexual copulation. No longer did he think with youthful negligence. His mind, body, and soul, loved this woman dangerously. Out there among the stars he fought the on-coming presence of closure. It was beginning to be difficult controlling the in-coming tide, but he couldn't help torqueing himself along her cavernous valley as she did her dirty little dance. He knew this drove her wild as much as it did him. The way her back would arch, the way she clawed at his chest, and the way she threw him in the wash cycle at the bottom of her stroke let him know this to be true.

The hour passed by without notice. The flames on the candles flickered dimly as they too, neared an inevitable end. A light sheen of perspiration coated their bodies leaving them glowing into the twilight of a new morning. The time had come for them to share with one another the libation of ritual.

"Give me love, Baby...come with me...My body craves your semen...Mmm...Oohh...Sss...Ahh."

Together they washed away any trace of uncertainty as they played curiously in their love. Bria looked down at Tywoun just as a tear escaped her eye, and said, "I dreamt of you for so long, before I even knew who you were...the way you would feel...the way you would love me tonight... There's nothing I can do to repay you for the way you make me feel – I love you, and I know that you may not feel as strongly as I do, but I promise to be true to you in your absence, just as I will in your presence. Sexually I will do whatever it is you ask. You're my king, and I'm here to serve you, just treat me as your Black Queen, and give me back what no other can Baby...Love! I can see forever in your eyes, and when you hold me close I feel at home close to your heart...Baby I know I'm rambling I just – "Ssshhh...I'm yours now and forever you are my Queen. Now allow me to take control of your body," as he rolled over on top of her.

"What about work?" Bria asked.

"Baby, I'm putting in overtime right now." Tywoun replied.

"OOOOOOO..."

15 THE TRUE MORNING AFTER

Lisa awoke from her mid-afternoon slumber to find herself alone. Shielding her eyes from the obtrusive pacific sun, she surveyed the area for any sign of Rick. Lisa stepped down from the hammock to take a closer look, still no sign of Rick. "He must be inside," she told herself.

"Rick, honey!" Lisa called.

No answer.....

"Rick, baby, where are you?"

Still no answer....

Curious as to where he may have gone; Lisa went into the parlor to see if Rick had left a note on the bar for her. To her surprise there was no note. "Hmm…that's odd! No big thing, he probably went for a walk." Lisa decided to wash away the light film of sweat clinging to her like a sticky glaze. By then she hoped Rick would have returned back by then.

Rejuvenated, Lisa applied the coconut oil (made fresh by the locals), to her satiny smooth skin. She loved the way it moisturized deep within her skin, leaving her body to feel as soft as a baby. She also loved the way it smelled on her, so fresh and clean. After dressing into her clothing, she decided to take a walk down to the beach to see if she could spot Rick hanging out. Once she arrived to her destination, she noticed there was no Rick to be found. Lisa was slowly becoming concerned. She looked down at her watch, it was a quarter pass three; an hour had passed. This was uncharacteristic of Rick to be gone this long without checking in, no note, call, or anything. Lisa's nerves were working on her conscious. She tried to remain calm, and re-enforce her confidence by telling herself, "Everything is fine, he'll be here shortly." Still the minutes ticked by in agonizing disbelief, as she watched helplessly when another hour passed.

Dusk was nearing its post, and Lisa was near panic. Back at the bungalow Lisa radioed the activities coordinator, Windell to see if perhaps the two had gone on another one of his famous treks. To no avail, he hadn't seen Rick since he had taken them snorkeling the day prior. Sensing a hint of hysteria in Lisa's voice, Windell assured her he would check with the other staff members, then he'd be over shortly, figuring she was in need of comforting.

Boy, did Rick have some explaining to do, but more importantly she just wanted to know that he was okay. She tried to settle her nerves by pouring herself a glass of wine. "No this isn't strong enough," she said, replacing the wine for a stronger glass of scotch. The first sip was like swallowing fire, as it burned its way down her throat taken her breath away. Unnervingly, Lisa polished off the first glass, and making no hesitation in helping herself to another.

"Darling!" Windell shouted from the door.

"Rick is that you?" Lisa shouted.

"Sorry Madam, it's just me, Windell."

He stated letting himself in. "I've called around, and Mr. Moss hasn't been seen by personnel all evening Luv, but I assure you there's no need to worry, maybe he's off clearing his mind. We really do have some majestic sights that's been known to hold a person's imagination. I'm sure he's fine, but here, let me get that glass from you my Queen. The last thing Mr. Moss needs is to find you wasted, and unable to enjoy your last night here in paradise." Windell said, relieving Lisa of her drink.

"Windell this is just not like him. I think we should send a search team out to look for him." Lisa rambled starting to feel the effects of the scotch.

"Now, now, my dear. I don't think that is necessary. Let's give it some time, I'm sure he'll show shortly, trust me." Windell comforted.

"How can you sit here calm like you are, when my man is missing?" Lisa shouted at Windell in anger.

"Mrs. Moss, please – you must remain level headed during this time."

"Come in Windell" came a voice across the radio he had hooked onto his belt.

"Windell speaking, go ahead." Windell stated into his radio.

"Windell what's your twenty?"

"I'm over here at Evuevu, Kemo, over!" Windell answered.

"Quick, ask him has he located Rick." Lisa ordered.

"Shhh…"Windell cut her off.

"Don't shush me!" Lisa yelled, pissed.

"Windell, when you're through there, could you stop by the Banquet Hall sir? There's something I think you need to see, over."

"Will do, over." Windell replied.

"Mrs. Moss, I have to make a run, you're more than welcome to join me if you would like, who knows, we might run into your mate."

"Okay, I'll go with you, but if we haven't heard from my baby by then promise me you'll send someone to look for him." Lisa bartered.

"You have my word, Luv." Windell agreed.

On the short ride over to the Banquet Hall, Lisa was totally silent assuming the worst had happened to Rick. As they approached closer to their designation, Lisa could smell the aroma of some unknown deliciousness carried by the cool night breeze, and she heard what had sounded to be a live band playing gregariously just over the hill. The last thing Lisa needed was to be surrounded by a celebration. All she wanted was her Rick, but she vowed to strangle him for scaring her half to death when he did surface.

"I don't mean to be inconsiderate, but could you hurry up?" Lisa said, as Windell exited the vehicle.

"Sure thing!" he replied.

A few moments later Lisa's heart burst with a tremendous amount of excitement. To her surprise, Rick stood a few hundred feet safe and sound holding a bouquet of assorted roses in one hand, and a sign which read: "Don't Be Mad, Please – Will you Marry Me?......."

Rick then dropped to one knee setting aside the flowers and sign, placing one of his hands into his pant pockets, he pulled out what looked to Lisa as a ring box. She couldn't get the car door opened quickly enough, so she could run down the aisle to him, her soon to be husband.

"Yes baby, yes, yes, yes!" Lisa answered emphatically as the tears flowed down her angelic face.

On cue Windell, Kemo and the entire resort staff appeared from their hiding spots in celebratory fashion, throwing handfuls of flower petals, and blowing kazoos.

"You scared me to death!" Lisa cried, punching rick playfully on his arm.

"I'm sorry Baby, but this was the way I had things arranged before we came over here. I wanted to make our last night the best night of our lives. Did I succeed?" Rick asked, while smiling.

"Yes Baby! I will never forget this night. I love you." Lisa replied, falling to her knees wrapping Rick in a loving embrace.

"I love you too, and I plan to spend the rest of my life showing you just how much I love you."

"I know you will baby, now let your fiancé see the ring you got her." Lisa said with a radiant smile on her face.

"Oh, my God!" Lisa exclaimed as her mouth dropped open.

It was a Cartier designed ten karat engagement ring made of clear V.V.S. diamonds; embedded on premium platinum, with ruby flakes accented throughout the band.

"Oh Rick, it's beautiful, very beautiful! Can I put it on now?"

"I thought you'd never ask." Rick stated, as he slid the ring up her slender finger.

"I love you, I love you, I love you, I love you, I love you..." Lisa stated, as she kissed him feverishly.

"Congratulations, you two!" Windell said, drawing their attention.

"You knew the whole time, you're very good Windell." Lisa said, shaking her head while smiling.

"I'm sorry Madam, but scout's honor are still scout's honor." Windell responded, signaling with a wink.

"We'll be heading out now, enjoy, and remember: Love lies in the strength of your bond. Cheerio! Come on gang let's leave these two to bask in their love."

It was a night soon not forgotten. For good reason, after being fed the most exquisite five course meal, they danced to the house band's rendition of Luther Vandross', 'If This World Were Mine." Then Rick romantically washed Lisa's feet in a nearby brook, while serenading her under the moonlight.

"Windell was right, the stars are gorgeous out here." Lisa said, looking to the sky.

"Why don't we see if what Windell said, about making love outside under the stars is better?" Rick replied.

"Do me right!" Lisa quipped.

They began to make infinity love beneath the stars, as they anticipated greeting the morning sunrise.

What a beautiful sunrise it will be.......

16 MAKING IT FINAL

"They'll be here any minute – Oooh, there they are now. Bria, over here!" Lisa shouted.

"So, how was Fiji?" Bria asked, as they embraced.

"Fiji was so beautiful, and look-" Lisa declared.

"Oh my; Lisa it's beautiful! So, when is the big date?" Bria asked.

"We haven't decided yet, come on, I want you to meet my fiancé." Lisa stated showingly.

"I'm sorry, Tywoun this is my BFF, Lisa Hamilton; Lisa this is the love of my life," Bria stated while introducing the two.

"Nice to have finally met you Tywoun, I've heard so much about you." Lisa stated.

"I've also heard so much about you as well, it's a pleasure, and congratulations on the engagement." Tywoun responded.

"Rick's waiting in a booth by the bar for us, come on, he's been waiting to meet the two of you." Lisa stated, while leading the way.

"Bri, Bri, you weren't lying, he does look like Tyson Beckford." Lisa stated, as they continued walking toward Rick.

"I look like Tyson Beckford?" Tywoun said sarcastically.

"Better Baby!" Bria exclaimed!

"And at last we meet Bria and Tywoun, how's it going? Rick greeted. "Congratulations!"

"The champagne is cold, how about we celebrate!" Rick said, popping the cork.

"Umm, Tywoun doesn't drink." Bria said, uneasily.

"No problem, he can have whatever he would like, it's on me." Rick concurred.

"So Lisa, tell me all the juicy details." Bria stated, giving Lisa one of their looks with a smile.

"While they discuss girl things, how about you and I, Tywoun shoot a couple games of pool?" Rick suggested to Tywoun.

"Rack'em up!" Tywoun replied.

"Ladies enjoy. Tywoun and I are going to shoot a few games," stated Rick.

*****

"So Tywoun, Lisa told me you just got out recently. How has your transition been so far? Rick asked.

"I've adjusted." Tywoun answered, shocked by Rick's audacity.

"I only ask, because I own an office business, and I'm in need of a Rep. Agent to handle urban affairs." Rick cleared the air as he could tell the aura had changed a bit.

"I just got a promotion at the steel plant, besides, I don't have much office experience." Tywoun responded.

"Starting pay starts at about a hundred grand a year, and you won't have to worry that much as the office work is very simple; more importantly you possess an unobtainable skill, and that's savvy street smarts. So, what will it be eight ball, call your shot, or loser rack?" Rick made an irrefutable offer.

"Eight ball will be fine. A hundred a year, huhn?" Tywoun said, quizzically.

"We'll have time for that later, right now, I'm about to school you!" Rick added with a smile on his face.

*****

"Girl let me tell you, the trip was well worth it, but sex on the beach is way over-rated, ha, ha, ha…" Lisa retorted in a show of gesture.

"You are one crazy nut, seriously crazy." Bria stated emphatically as she sipped her drink.

"Burnt hell, you see what it's like with sand up the crack of your ass." Lisa exaggerated.

"Ha, ha, ha…I'm glad you're happy and I'm sorry for your raw behind. Aren't you happy you let love re-enter your life?" Bria asked.

"You know Bri, for a long time I was afraid to let myself fall in love, and on the other hand I felt it would be wrong to give my love to another man, but deep down Bri I've longed for so long to love, and to be loved whole-heartedly in return. Meeting Rick has brought new meaning to my life and, and…" Lisa broke off her sentence as her words became muffled.

"Awe…don't cry, you'll ruin your mascara and be all ugly! Now stop before you make me cry- see what you did? Now I'm crying!" Bria said, as she wiped at the tears falling from her eyes.

"Bri, I want to thank you for truly being my best friend." Lisa expressed sincerely.

"You don't have to thank me Lisa, you know that you are my sister, and I want to see you happy. Now give me a hug, then let's head to the ladies room to fix ourselves back up." Bria said, with a big smile.

"I love you, Bri." Lisa replied.

I love you too. So, am I the maid of honor or what?" Bria questioned playfully.

"Wench, stop playing, you know you are! Come on, let's go get freshened up."

"Okay, but first let's go tell the guys." Bria replied, as they got up to walk toward the guys to let them know where they were going.

*****

"Get your hand off me!" Bria shouted angrily, as some guy grabbed her as she and Lisa were leaving the restroom.

"Ay shorty, I just want to talk."

"I'm sorry, but I have a man, now turn me loose!" Bria pulled away impatiently.

"Brother you're messing with the wrong one, now let her go." Lisa stepped in.

"So what's up; y'all diking? Stop cock blocking bitch, and move on." Dude spat.

"Bitch! Bitch! I got your bitch!" Lisa replied angrily.

"I'm only telling you this one more time, take your hating ass on bitch!" he warned...

"Ay homeboy, take your hands off the woman. I'm only asking you once." Tywoun appeared up like some type of magic.

"Nigga you better get your captain save-a-hoe ass away from me."

On instinct Tywoun punched the dude in the face, causing him to fall to the ground.

"No, Tywoun! Stop! He's not worth it baby." Bria pleaded.

"Yea man, she's right, let it go." Rick said, as he grabbed Tywoun pulling him back from attacking the guy again.

"We're going to finish this after the club superman," the guy stated, grinning while getting up off the ground. As he wiped the trickle of blood from his lip.

"Black folks always know how to mess something up; that was unnecessary." Lisa spoke as she shook her head.

"Tell me about it." Rick seconded.

"Tywoun baby, calm down, please just let it go. Look at me baby; I'm fine, he didn't hurt me, can we please just let it go?" Bria pleaded.

"We can finish celebrating at my house." Rick suggested.

"No, I won't run from that clown. We came here tonight to enjoy ourselves, and no one should take that from us." Tywoun stated.

"Tywoun, baby, look at me." Bria said placing her hands on the side of his face, in hopes of calming him.

"Baby you have nothing to prove, can we go make the best of the night?" Bria said, reaching up hoping to lull his inner beast to sleep with a kiss.

"Clowns like that should pay." Tywoun stated.

"I know honey, but let someone else handle that, please can we go?" Bria pleading further.

"Okay", Tywoun finally agreed.

After collecting their things the four of them exited the club.

"Hey superman! Mr. Captain-save-a-ho! Catch this!" The familiar voice shouted from behind them.

"Get down, he has a gun!!!"

"Pop…Pop…Pop…Pop…Pop…" shots echoed through the air….

"Is everyone alright?" Rick asked, rolling off Lisa.

"I'm alright." Lisa answered.

"Bria, are you alright?" Lisa asked with concern.

"I think so." Bria responded.

"Tywoun, baby, Oh my God! Someone please call an ambulance, hurry! Baby, please hang on. Hurry! Someone please call an ambulance now! Tywoun, baby stay with me, keep your eyes open. No, Tywoun keep them open. Shh…Shh…Shh…don't speak, save your energy. I got you – someone please help.

17 THE STORM

At the hospital Lisa and Rick tried their best to console Bria. The moments dragged by in agony. Every second passed brought Bria's mind to an unfavorable conclusion. Blood and tears soaked her clothes from head to toe as she held Tywoun in her arms, willing him to be strong while she hummed a gospel hymn her late grandmother used to hum in the presence of tribulation. Bria's heart gaped with an enormous sense of separation. Just when love was to anoint her with its many blessings, life's cruelty thrust upon her a cross too heavy to shoulder. Bria etched a path in the floor as she paced back and forth. The sound of doors opening drew her attention hoping it was the doctor bearing good news.

With the oncoming of the hour; Bria's mind only wondered more and more. Is he alive? How bad is it? How will she tell his girls? Will God be so cruel? Bria couldn't understand why after her heart was apprehended for so long, now, just as her life was filled with vibrant color. Would her freedom of happiness be revoked for undisclosed reasoning? It just wasn't fair.

Bria sat helplessly as she waited for the medics to finish the emergency surgery.

"Lisa would you pray with me?" Bria asked, as she fought to hold back her tears.

"Yes baby, we can pray." Lisa replied to her best friend.

On bended knees Bria lead them in prayer.

"God, I know it's been sometime since we've spoke, but I really need you to listen to me right now. Please God; don't take Tywoun away from me. He is a changed man. He takes care of his kids, and he treats me like no other man has and for this I wish to spend the rest of my life with him. Taking him will leave me here lost and all alone. Please! Please God don't take my Tywoun…" Bria lost her last shred of resolve.

"Shh…shh…come here Bri." Lisa comforted her.

"Lisa I don't want to lose him." Bria whispered.

"I know Bri, I know, Tywoun is strong, he's going to pull through. Keep your faith Bri." Lisa encouraged.

Once Bria and Lisa finished praying, a female nurse entered the waiting room where they were. Before the nurse could get one word out of her mouth, Bria cut into her.

"Is Tywoun okay?!" Is he going to make it?!" Bria asked, with great concern.

"We're not sure yet, but I've come to tell you that there are two detectives here that would like to speak with you all." Stated the nurse.

It appeared that the detectives entered the room introducing themselves before the nurse could finish her statement.

"I'm Detective Tillery, and this is my partner, Detective Williams. We're here from the Quincy Police Department. We would like to ask you all a few questions about tonight's shooting."

"But first, could we get your names and relationships to the victim for our records?" Detective Williams asked.

They all gave the detectives their names and relationships to Tywoun.

"Does anyone here know why, or what led to Mr. Thomas getting shot tonight?" Detective Tillery asked.

"Ms. Lewis, you did state that you're Mr. Thomas girlfriend, correct?"

"Yes; that's correct." Bria responded

"Did he ever mention to you that he had any enemies, or any problems with anyone lately?"

"He never mentioned to me that he had any enemies, or problems with no one." Bria stated, as tears streamed down her face.

"Could anyone of you in your words tell us what happened inside the club tonight before Mr. Thomas got shot leaving the club?" Detective Williams asked.

"I…I…I mean we were…" Bria tried to speak, but her tears and pain wouldn't allow her to complete one sentence.

"It's okay Bri baby, I'll tell them." Lisa grabbed and hugged Bria.

"We went to the club just to have a nice time together, Tywoun and Rick were playing a game of pool. Bria and I were at the table sipping on our drinks while having some girl talk. For some silly reason we both shed some tears which made our makeup run. We decided to go to the restroom to freshen up. So, we walked over to the guys to tell them where we were going and that we'd be back shortly.

After about five minutes, or so, in the girls room Bri and I started to head back to the men before some other women grabbed them.

When we stepped out of the restroom door, we noticed some guys standing close by as we opened the door. One of the guys grabbed Bria by the arm, and said, what's up Ms. Sexy – am I the one you're looking for? Or something like that. Bri told him to please let her arm go, but he refused, that's when I jumped in and told him to let her go as she asked. He started calling me all kinds of vulgar names, and told me to mind my damn business…"

"Did you or Ms. Lewis know this guy?" Detective Tillery cut in and asked Lisa.

"No, we didn't." Lisa responded.

"Please continue with your story." Detective Williams stated.

"Like I said, he got real disrespectful toward me. I guess by then Ty and Rick noticed what was happening, so they came over to assist…

"Excuse me, who is Ty?" Detective Tillery stopped Lisa and asked her.

"Oh, that's what we call Tywoun sometimes." Lisa stated.

"Please continue." Detective Tillery told Lisa as he wrote a note in his notebook.

"So, like I was saying, Ty and Rick walked up, and Ty asked the guy to please let his girl's arm go. The guy started saying a bunch of crazy stuff, and the next thing I know the guy fell to the ground. Rick and the other guys standing around stepped in between Ty and the guy. When the guy got up from the floor, he said something like; I got something for you Superman, I got you Mr. Captain-Save-A-Ho.

Ty said, yeah, whatever dude and we all walked back to our table.

Once we got to the table, Bri stated that she wanted to leave because she had lost her groove, and wasn't feeling the spot anymore.

After we all discussed her request, we decided to gather our belongings and leave the place.

Once we got outside the club walking toward our cars; someone shouted hey 'Superman, I told you I had something for you…catch these Nigga.' I think it was Ty; somebody stated that he has a gun – get down!!! The next thing we heard was – pop, pop, pop, pop, pop. While on the ground, I heard someone say, let's get out of here before the police get here; and then I heard some tires peeling off.

Rick asked if everyone was okay, and everyone responded except Ty. That's when we discovered he had been shot and was bleeding badly." Lisa stopped talking as tears streamed down her face heavily.

Rick immediately stepped toward Lisa and put his arms around her and Bria assuring them that Tywoun is strong and he will pull through this situation.

"Well, I know it's going to be a long night for you all; I think Detective Williams and I have taken up enough of your time. Please take our cards, and if anyone of you happen to remember anything else about tonight, please let us know. Any information may help us identify the shooter, so please contact one of us immediately. Good night." Detective Tillery stated.

"And Ms. Lewis, providing that all turns out good for Mr. Thomas, and when he is able and feeling up to it...please have him call us...and, you all be strong, and have a good night." Detective Williams stated, as he and his partner turned to leave the room.

18 THE CALM AFTER THE STORM

After about three and a half hours, one of the doctors appeared through the door removing his gloves from his hands; looking as if he had come right off the battlefield. His body showing signs of wear and tear and his face showing exhaustion.

"Are you all Mr. Thomas' family?" The doctor asked Bria, Lisa and Rick.

"Yes! Is he okay?!...Please tell me he made it." Bria said, frantically.

"Ma'am Mr. Thomas has slipped into a coma, we have managed to sustain his life for now. But, for how long remains to be determined. The good news is, we were able to remove all three bullets lodged in his back. And as for the two shots in his right leg, the bullets went straight through, shattering his lower fibia; so, he's being fitted with a cast as we speak. He's a strong man, Ms., I think he will pull through. May I ask who you are to him?" The doctor asked Bria.

"I'm his girlfriend," Bria answered.

"Does he have any blood relatives?" He questioned further.

"He never spoke about his mother or father, but he does have two young children from a previous relationship." Bria replied.

"That's fine, I'll have you placed as his only known relative. This way you will have access to sensitive information if that's okay with you."

"Yes! That would be fine with me."

"Good, I'll be back shortly with a few forms I'll need you to read and sign, which will make you his beneficiary. I'll be right back. Do you have any questions for me?" The doctor asked her before he stepped away.

"When can I see him?" Bria asked.

"He'll be moved to his room soon as his cast is set. I'll send a nurse when he's ready. Is there anything else?" He asked.

"No, that's everything." Bria replied.

Somehow she felt relieved knowing that the immediate danger was over.

If she knew her Tywoun, she knew he would fight, because he has too much to live for. Then she thought to herself, who was going to tell his kids...."

"Who's going to tell Brittani and Elisa?" Bria blurted out loud.

"Who?" Lisa asked.

"Brittani and Elisa, Tywoun's daughters." Bria answered.

"I would think it would be best to tell their mother, and let her handle the sensitive matter." Lisa stated. "They're going to be so heartbroken. The both of them are so crazy about their Dad, he just re-entered their lives. He can't die, they need him." Bria spoke, as the tears began to swell back up in her eyes.

"Bri, is there anything we can do for you?" Lisa asked.

"Thank you Lisa, but there's nothing right now. Why don't you two go home and get some rest." Bria answered.

"Are you sure there's nothing you need us to handle?" Lisa asked further.

"I'm sure, I'll call you if I do. I'm waiting here until I can go see him, then I'm going home to shower and change. Hopefully, by then the sun will be rising; so I can go by his kids' mother's house to inform her of what has happened. After that, I'm coming back to the hospital to be by his side." Bria answered.

"Well call me if you need anything, okay? I'll come back by here after work." Lisa said, while hugging Bria.

"Bria it's been a pleasure meeting you, and I'm sorry about tonight. If there's anything I can do just ask, and don't worry about the cost of this; it's all covered." Rick stated.

"Thank you Rick. I'll talk to you guys later." Bria finished.

"Bye, don't forget to call me, for anything." Lisa said, as she and Rick headed out the hospital.

"I won't." Bria replied.

19 COMING CLEAN, BEARING IT ALL

"Who is it?" Sharice asked, as she made her way to the door.

"It's Bria, Sharice can I speak with you for a moment?" Bria answered.

"Yes, what is it?" Snapped Sharice.

"The kids aren't around are they?"

"No, why is that any of your concern?" Sharice snapped again.

"What I have to tell you, you will need to tell them." Bria paused.

"Tell them what?! Sharice asked getting more impatient.

"Tywoun was shot five times last night, and he's in a coma. They don't know if he's going to make it." Bria said, trying not to cry.

"So, that life finally caught up with him." Sharice stated callously.

"How could you sit there and say something like that, he's done nothing since he's been out, but spend time with his kids. He loves them more than life, and to go back to the way his life was before hasn't been a thought in his mind. I have you to know that he has exceeded everyone's expectations; I see now, even yours. He already had it hard enough having to deal with the authorities, and those in the streets that used to know him, for you too, to stand against him." Bria said, angered by Sharice's lack of compassion.

"And who are you supposed to be?!" Sharice retaliated.

"I'm the woman that believes in him. He's at Blessing Hospital, room #222, 4th floor. You should take the girls to see him, if he hears their voices, it may give him the strength to come back to us. Have a nice day." Bria spoke with pride, turning away making her way to her car. Once inside the car, she broke all to pieces as she thought of the pain the girls will endure. The insensitivity of their mother made her cringe even more. Bria didn't know the situation between Tywoun and his baby mama, but what she did know was no problem should make a person that bitter.

*****

107

Back at the hospital, Bria sat beside Tywoun holding his hand in hers as she thought of how much he truly meant to her, and how much joy he had added to her life. There was nothing more she wanted than for him to open his eyes, and say Baby let's go home. Bria kept negative thoughts far from her mind. Her strength was his strength, and she spoke words of empowerment to him knowing he was listening. "You can beat this Ty, fight, and come back to us. We need you Ty, fight, fight baby, I'm right here with you."

There was a soft tap on the door....

"Come in." Bria announced. Sharice entered the room with Brittani and Elise by her side. The children's emotions began to run rampant at the sight of their father lying in the hospital bed. Tubes coming from his nose and mouth, not to mention the ones in his arms.

"Daddy! Daddy! Bria please help him, don't let him die." Brittani cried out.

"Yeah Daddy, please don't leave us. I promise to be good, just don't leave." Elisa sobbed her little plea.

"I'm going to the cafeteria so you can all be alone. Is there anything I can get you?" Bria

asked, trying not to break down in front of them.

"Bria help my daddy, make him all better." Brittani ran into her arms.

"Please Bria, fix him up for us, so he can be with us, and make him better." Elisa poured her little heart out.

"Girls your Dad is strong, he's fighting; together we all have to be strong, and fight with him. Okay?" Bria spoke with what little resolve she had left.

"Bria, I wanna fight whoever hurt my daddy." Elisa said, wiping at the tears that was were running down her face.

"I know baby, just be strong for your father." Bria said, kneeling down to give her a hug.

"Okay." Elisa answered, before sniffling as she fought to stop crying.

As Bria turned to leave the room, she noticed Sharice appeared to be outside her callous exterior and that she was hurting as well; no amount of anger could cover that up.

"Now would be the best time to get that weight off your chest." Bria advised Sharice.

"I don't know what to say." Sharice whispered.

"Open your heart, and let the words out. He's been waiting for you to talk to him."

"Yeah mama! Daddy said, you will always be special to him." Elisa expressed.

"Talk to him mama." Brittani pleaded.

"Come on girls, let you mom talk to your father. Let's say we get us some ice cream. How does that sound?" Bria asked.

"Can we get Daddy one too?" Elisa asked, innocently.

"Dad can't eat anything right now Sissy." Brittani replied.

"We can save it for him. He's going to be hungry when he wakes up, right Bria?" Elise's questions tore through Bria's heart as she succumbed to the somber mood taking over the room. Quickly she refocused, patting the corners of her blood shot eyes.

"Come on girls, I'm ready." Bria said, taking a deep breath.

"You two behave." Sharice ordered.

"Yes Ma'am!" They both said in unison.

…Sharice approached the bed where Tywoun laid unconscious with an uneasy hesitation. The sound of the ventilator hissing created an almost sinister chorus of assisted breaths, while the heart monitor beeped adding to the eerie mystique.

"Tywoun, I know you can hear me…I'm sorry for everything, I – I thought of you every day for a few years, but it was all about the streets with you Tywoun. You never took a moment to think about what it would do to me if something were to happen to you. For months, I sat useless for those around me, including myself. Then one day, I woke up and in my mind I resented all that you were. I thought how could you leave me five months pregnant with twins, and no money? Every Ho you were messing with had something of yours, but all I had was your children growing in my womb. How could you leave me like that? I begged and pleaded. We was supposed to be a family, and family don't abandon one another. The only way I could deal with the pain was to tell myself I hated you, but how could I hate you when every day that passed your little ones grew to look more and more like you. Do you know how hard it is to comfort a child that asks daily; "Mama, why don't my daddy want to see me?" There's not a worse feeling than to hear how the other kids be picking on your kids, calling them bastards, or telling them their father don't love them, and that's why he left. If you only feel a fraction of my pain. You would know that me and the girls were locked up with you too, you weren't the only one incarcerated. We, your family, also sat in a cell deprived of a freedom of being a family. Your decisions caused you to get locked up, but me and the kids didn't get to make a choice. I felt like you chose the life of the streets over your family. So, I decided to let the streets be the one to worry about you, to keep you informed, and to make sure you had what you need. I hope now you see that the streets are illusions that don't love you back…

Tywoun, I'm glad to see you doing good for yourself, and being a father to our children. They worship the ground you walk on. Brittani is so much like you. She even sleep with her arm over her head like you used to. Elisa, well she has my personality, but your charisma, and if you let her, she will tell you about her dad all day long. Tywoun they really need you. I need you. Be strong and pull through this situation, we're counting on you…"

*****

"Is Daddy going to be alright?" Brittani asked. "Daddy is strong sissy – he has superpowers." Elisa said, licking her ice cream cone. "Yeah, Brittani your father is very strong. How is your ice cream?" Bria asked, trying to lighten the mood.

"I don't want Daddy to leave us." Brittani spoke, solemnly.

"Me either." Elisa seconded.

"Bria why would anyone want to hurt my Daddy?" Brittani questioned with a childhood innocence.

"You have some bad people in the world who sometimes don't care who they hurt, or understand their actions in certain situations." Bria answered.

"Is Daddy a bad person?" Elisa cut in.

"No Baby! He's a wonderful man who once made a few bad decisions when he was younger that's all. He loves you and your sister very much, he wouldn't do anything to jeopardize being separated from you two again." Bria answered.

"Can we go back now?" Brittani asked, as she tried to finish her ice cream.

"Yes Baby, we can go back in just a second." Bria stated.

*****

"Mama, we back!" Brittani announced.

Sharice had been crying, and she made no attempt to hide it. She had finally spoken what she had kept inside of her for so long which had made her so bitter toward Tywoun. She was finally able to remove her bitterness and exhale.

Bria and the kids all grabbed a seat with Sharice, they comforted one another while they waited and kept their fingers crossed that Tywoun would awaken soon. The hours crept by bringing nightfall. The kids began to tire, so Bria suggested to Sharice to take them home and get some much needed rest. She told her she would keep her posted; so it would be no need for her to worry.

Sharice took Bria's advice, and told the girls to gather their things. They all hugged Bria, said their good nights and headed out the room.

After they left, Bria decided to lay on a cot that was near Ty's bed. She laid there listening to the rasp of the ventilator until she fell asleep...

20 HIDDEN BLESSING

Bria's gaze held transfixed in a world that belonged all to her while the rain beat at the window pane in a soothing rhythm. It's been two months and there was no signs of coming change. Still Bria kept her faith in God, and the strength of her man. She had to take an indefinite leave from her job, which was something her boss, Mr. Sanders' encouraged. The daily routine of the doctors and nurses had become all too familiar. Bria even gave Tywoun a sponge bath daily. In her mind they shared these intimate moments together. She was sure of it, because his hard-on told her so. Bria tried it all; she pleasured her man, she prayed over her man, she all but sold her soul to the devil. The latter was negotiable for the warmth of his embrace.

Lisa, Sharice and the kids were there frequently. The kids had even kept Bria company many nights, giving her a reason to smile. Daily, the kids would give Tywoun a rundown of their day hoping he was listening. Bria was almost positive he felt their presence. She noticed when they would talk to him, or just be present his heart rate would accelerate almost to say, "I hear you, Daddy hears you."

Taken from her thoughts, Bria was startled by rummaging. Looking around the darkened room it was just him and her. "Must be a mouse," she told herself. Again, there it was the same sound, now it was the sound of crinkling sheets. When it finally registered Bria bolted for the lights hoping her prayers had finally been answered. Once she got the lights on, she noticed that Tywoun's hands were showing signs of life grabbing at the crisp linen sheets. His eyes flutter as if reliving a nightmare that somehow wouldn't loosen its grip on his mind, refusing to let him wake up.

"Tywoun! Baby! Wake up! Wake up Baby. Fight it Tywoun!" Bria coached continuously.

The sandman released Tywouns mind and his body as well.

"Bria…"he spoke barely above an audible.

"Yes baby! I'm here, I'm here Tywoun, just save your strength." Bria answered excitedly.

"Brit-Brit El, Eli" Tywoun's voice trailed off.

"The girls, they're fine. They've been here every night talking to you Baby." Bria stated.

Tears fell from Tywoun's eyes as he took a deep breath. Bria placed her hand inside his transferring her unwavering strength. Pressing the button to the nurses' station Bria alerted the nurses. Then she called Sharice and announced the good news. In seconds the room was filled with doctors, and nurses moving frantically as they checked Tywoun's vital signs.

Within ten minutes Sharice and the girls rushed through the door. A great sense of relief infected all those who stood in wait for two long miserable months. The doctors asked that everyone who wasn't a member of the medical staff to please leave the room. They needed to thoroughly examine Mr. Thomas.

Once outside in the hallway, Bria and Sharice embraced one another as the tears – not of sorrow; but that of jubilation poured freely. The two women became an unforeseen pair, understanding what matters the most, the kids; and the relationship they share in correspondence with what mattered.

"Come Babies." Bria turned toward Brittani and Elisa pulling them closer to her and their mother to form a newly circle of trust, love and family.

"God answered our prayers didn't he; Mama?" Brittani asked.

"Yes Baby! He answered your prayers, all of our prayers." Sharice answered.

"God is good!" Elisa quipped.

"Amen!" they all replied in unison before making laughter fill the room.

21 HE'S COMING BACK

After a month of rehabilitation Tywoun was finally cleared to leave the hospital. Bria told him that she refused to let him out of her sight, she had already gathered his things from his place and moved them to her house; she wasn't going to have it no other way – end of conversation.

His daughters were happy and in good spirits again, they couldn't wait to start helping their dad with as much as they could. Plus their parents had finally sat with each other and came to grips with their past; freeing one another from their regrets and resentment.

Despite the slight limp in Tywoun's left leg, his wounds were healing pretty well. Not yet at 100%, but he was regaining his strength gradually.

"Are you ready to go Mr. Thomas?" the nurse stated, while standing at the door.

"Yes, I just need to grab a few more things, then I'll be ready." He replied.

"Ms. Lewis just called and said she'd be here shortly." The nurse relayed.

"Okay; thank you!" He said, with a big smile on his face.

Alone with his own thoughts Tywoun contemplated his final moments playing out right before his eyes. There stood a pain stricken Bria crying over his lifeless body, asking the Lord to please save him. Just to her right Sharice tried consoling the kids, because they couldn't understand why their father had to go so soon after coming into their lives. Tywoun looked to his right, and saw the doctors telling their assistants they've done all they could do, besides wait and pray for the best.

Was this God's way of freeing him fully of the devil's grip? Bringing Tywoun to a full understanding of life, love, and a second chance.

"Hey Baby! Are you ready to go home?" Bria broke through his thoughts.

Shaking free of the subjective scene created by his mind, he turned toward her and said; "Yes Queen let's go home."

"Let me help you. I have the car waiting at the front door." Bria said, putting his arm across her shoulder.

"Bria, I just want to say that; I love you, and thanks for not giving up on me." Tywoun stopped to look into her eyes to show her just how much it meant to him.

"Love conquers all things, and together we're going to make it through this situation. Now, give me a kiss and let's get you out of here; let's go home. The girls have something special in store for you, so let's go." Bria replied flicking off the light as she followed him out the room.

On the short ride home, Tywoun looked out at life enjoying its simplicity, for he truly was happy to be alive, and loved.

"We're here! Is everything okay?" Bria asked, showing a concern.

"It couldn't be better." Tywoun answered, with a super smile on his face.

"Good, well let's not keep the girls waiting. They really worked hard putting their plan together, I know you're going to like it." Bria said, as she opened the car door.

"Surprise!!!" Brittani, Elisa, Sharice, Lisa, Rick and Shyheed all stood applauding Tywoun's triumphant victory.

"Thank you all, you're too kind." Tywoun filled up with joy and a sense of belonging.

"Welcome home Daddy!" Brittani and Elisa rejoiced before running into his arms.

"It's good to be home. You two put this together; what does that banner say? World Greatest Dad!" Tywoun read.

"You're the bestest Daddy ever."

Brittani said, hugging him even tighter.

"Yea bestest ever, Dad!" Elisa seconded.

"Wait till you see what they prepared for you." Sharice stated, with a smile.

"Come on Daddy, we bake a cake for you." The girls pulled him into the house and into the dining room where a vanilla cake covered in strawberries, which was their Dad's favorite fruit, there were also a few presents, and two letters which were written and signed by the girls.

"Mommy and Bria helped us Daddy. Go ahead and open your presents." Brittani said, handing him her gift.

Opening the gift, it was coffee mug with, "World's Greatest Dad," engraved on it.

"I can definitely use this for my morning coffee, thank you Baby." Tywoun said.

"Open mine Daddy!" Elisa said with excitement while handing him another gift which felt like a shirt.

After he opened it, he started smiling holding it up in front of him. On front of the shirt there was a picture of his girls, Brittani and Elisa smiling.

"Look on the back Daddy!" Elisa said.

On the back it read: "I love My Dad!"

"I love both presents and I love you two so much, thank you both." Tywoun said, giving them each a big hug.

Next he opened the first letter which was from Brittani. It read:

"Dear Dad...

I hope when you read this letter you are all better. I'm so happy you are my Daddy. You always spend time with me and Elisa, and you listen to me. Dad I prayed to Heaven every night, well me and Elisa, before we went to bed. We asked God to let you be our Dad, because you are my best friend – o, you and Elisa to she's my bestest sissy. You're the best Daddy ever.

Love you...

Brittani"

"Read mine Daddy!" Elisa said, handing him her letter. It read:

"Dear Daddy...

I love you Daddy, you are so cool. When I tell all my friends about you they tell me you're the coolest. I think you are a superhero. Do you have super powers like Superman Daddy? If you two get in a fight I know you will win. Daddy will you wake up now? I want to play with you. Do you want to play with me too? I can't wait for you to wake up. I even asked Jesus to wake you up, but he never answered me back. He never answers me. I even promised I be good, and not get smart with Brittani. It's been hard Daddy, cuz Brittani can get on your nerves sometimes, but I love my sissy. Wake up Daddy so we can play, Bye Elisa...

O, and I love you!"

Tywoun couldn't hold back the tears that rolled down his face. And he made no attempts to wipe them away.

"You two are the reason I live. My world resolves around you two, and I'll never choose anything before family again. I have all I need in this room; family and good friends. Rick, Lisa thank you for being there that means so much to me. Shyheed, you've always been my man, a brother from another mother – I love you.

Sharice, the mother of our two beautiful daughters. None of this would be the same if you weren't included. I'm glad you, me and Bria can co-exist without conflict. Thank you so much.

Bria, baby; where do I start? My guardian angel, my light, my love. Since meeting you my life's been nothing but better. You are an amazing woman. There's no limit of my appreciation for you, and all that you do. To all of you, I heard your prayers, and I want y'all to know that they helped see me through. Now, can I have a slice of this delicious looking creation in front of me?"

Everyone enjoyed a slice of the mouth-watering cake while discussing nothing in particular. Laughter filled the room after months of pain and sorrow. Things couldn't be better. As the evening carried on Tywoun couldn't wait for when he could share some alone time with Bria. It had been over three months since he last swam in what she referred to as her sun warmed stream.

"We better get going." Lisa said, as she stood up grabbing for her belongings.

"Stay for dinner." Bria invited.

"Thank you, but Rick and I already made plans for tonight." Lisa answered.

"I should be getting the girls home too." Sharice said, gathering their things.

"Daddy can we stay here tonight with you and Bria?" Elisa asked.

"Dad needs his rest, and he probably wants to spend time alone with Bria, right Dad?" Brittani said, knowingly.

"Yes Baby, I do need my rest and I would like to spend tonight with Bria if that's alright with you two?" Tywoun replied.

"Daddy you wanna play kissy face with Bria again don't you?" Elisa asked in her usual candor.

"Girl, come on here with your crazy self." Sharice stated, not at all surprised as the remarks Elisa made.

"What am I going to do with you baby girl?" Tywoun said, with a laugh.

"Bye Dad." Brittani said giving him a hug.

"I'll be to get you two tomorrow, we'll go do something together okay?" Tywoun replied.

"Can we go to the mall?" Elisa asked.

"Yes we can go to the mall baby, now be good and listen to your mother." Tywoun answered.

"Bye Daddy!" Elisa shouted in excitement.

"Thank you Bria." Sharice spoke, opening the door to leave.

"You're welcome, and don't forget to call me." Bria responded.

"Well Ty and Bria, I think my time has come too, I'm going to tail Sharice and my nieces to make sure they get home safe and I need to go handle some biz." Shyheed stated, before he gave Tywoun a hug and headed for the door.

"So Rick, have you guys set a date for the wedding?" Tywoun asked.

"Matter-a-fact we were waiting for you to get better, because I want you to be one of my groomsmen." Rick replied.

"Word! Thank you, I'd like that." Tywoun exclaimed.

"Any man that would give his life to save another's life is truly a friend of mine." Rick said, giving Tywoun some dap.

"We were thinking around the third week in August." Lisa revealed.

"That's only a month away." Bria jumped in.

"Don't worry we covered all bases. All that's left for us to do is have everybody fitted for their dresses, and tuxedos." Lisa said, easing Bria's tension.

"Relax, trust us everything is going to be perfect. Enjoy the rest of your evening we will fill you in on all the details later. Come on Lisa let's leave these two to themselves." Rick said, as they walked toward the door to leave.

"Now that it's just us two, how about we get you out of them clothes, so I can see if I still got it." Tywoun spoke pulling his shirt off.

"What about your bullet wounds?" Bria asked, as she rubbed over his bandages.

"I thought maybe you could rub over them, while I make love to you." Tywoun states, as he nibbled on her neck.

"Mmm…come on Baby, do me right." Bria replied, lost in the heat of the moment.

22 PREPARING FOR FOREVER

While the women are out getting fitted why don't you and I grab a bite to eat?" Rick suggested to Tywoun.

"How does Kelly's sound? We can grab a bite while we discuss our future." Rick said.

"I'm game." Tywoun accepted the offer.

Tywoun had gained all of his strength back in his left leg, he no longer needed a walking cane to assist him. It felt good to be able to get back to his regular life. Life was wonderful, and it only seem to be getting better as each day passed.

After being seated the two ordered porterhouse steaks, with home fries for their sides. While waiting for their orders to arrive, the two discussed Rick's upcoming nuptials between him and Lisa.

"Can I ask you something Rick?" Tywoun questioned.

"Anything." Rick answered, tearing into his juicy steak the waitress just placed before him.

"When did you know that you wanted to spend the rest of your life with Lisa, at what moment did it become evidently clear that there was no questioning love?" Tywoun asked, dropping a heavy one on Rick.

"I think I know where this is going, but I'll humor you. When I first met Lisa it was all carnal energy. I mean a lust so powerful it consumed all reasoning and twisted all logic. It was only supposed to be physical, we both agreed in the beginning. Then I found myself needing that energy, her energy, and our sexual tryst did nothing to answer this calling for a more monogamous bonding of divine intervention. I knew Lisa felt just as I did, it was present in her touch and in the way she looked at me, but something which was unknown to me at time scared her from allowing the strong force within her to live. So naturally she goes on to wing herself off of me; not returning my calls, always too busy to see me. Now I never been one to seat over nothing but the heat, but Brother Tywoun, when I tell you I had it bad, I mean bad. I mean not wanting to wash your ass kind of bad. It was in that moment of desperation when I came to understand the feeling that I felt, I understood it would do one or two things. One; it would keep me stuck in a rut, or two; it would show me the fabric of love's design. For my sake, it was the second option that prevailed in the end. I mean in that moment I cared about nothing except her happiness, and I wanted to be the one to see that every day of our lives I was the one who brought said happiness to her. Never give up, or give in on love Tywoun. There's something mystical in its powers, and it's that much more majestic when the two of you see it together." Rick dropped knowledge.

"Man, that's deep. I understand now what love truly is, and I can honestly say I know what I want." Tywoun expressed openly.

"How old are you Tywoun?" Rick asked.

"I'm 28." He replied.

"See, I have you by years, but mentally you and I are one in the same. So, when are you going to ask her?" Rick drawing his own conclusion.

"I don't even have a ring yet."

"Don't worry about that, when we leave here I'll take you to my jeweler, and have him show you some engagement and wedding sets. Cool?" Rick offered.

"I-I can't afford a ring right now." Tywoun answered unashamedly.

"Nothing to worry about, I'll take care of it for you." Rick declared.

"I can't let you do that, you just covered my hospital bill Rick, I"

"That's what friends are for, to help one when it is needed if they are able to, don't look at it as a handout, me just giving you money. I'm hoping that you'll be my new Urban Affairs Rep. That way you and I can work out an arrangement for a payment plan, and you won't feel like I'm stunting on you. I guess what I need to be asking you is one: would you like to join me and my company? I can truly use you with your experience, and two; are you ready to give unconditionally and work relentlessly to keep the love exciting? If so, then we need to go see my jeweler." Rick said, setting his fork and steak knife across his plate.

"You think your jeweler will be willing to assist us on such short notice?" Twoun asked.

"That's not a problem — waiter!" Rick yelled as he dialed the jeweler's number.

"Yes," the waiter answered as she walked over to the table.

"Could you have this wrapped for me, and bring the check please?" Rick stated.

*****

That looks good on you Bria. So, how has Tywoun's recovery come along?" Lisa ran off as she complimented Bria on her bridesmaid gown.

"He's doing great. He doesn't need the assistance of a cane anymore. Does this dress make my butt look too big?" Bria shot back as she posed in the mirror.

"Humongous." Lisa teased.

"Forget you hussy, my man can't seem to get enough of my big butt." Bria shot back shaking her hips from side to side.

"It's good to see you happy Bri, you two are right for one another, and that's special. Hold on to him Bri, guys like Rick and Tywoun come only once in a lifetime. So keep him close to your heart." Lisa shared a moment of truth.

"Look at you Ms.- A man has no room in my heart; just in my bed. You've really become a love specialist. I'm impressed." Bri, true love – I mean, true feel-it-deep-down-in-your-soul-love is rarely found once it's lost. Don't sleep on true love is all I'm saying." Lisa confided.

"If I didn't know any better, I'd say you were trying to get me to marry Tywoun." Bria replied.

"And if he asked, would you accept his proposal?" Lisa asked.

"Of course I would – in a heartbeat." Bria answered without any thought.

"Good answer." Lisa stated.

"By the way hussy, so when were you going to tell me you were pregnant, you heifer?" Lisa questioned with contempt.

"How could you tell? I'm still trying to accept the fact that I'm going to be a mommy and here it is you already know." Bria said, with surprised conviction.

"When have you ever been able to hide anything from me Bri, besides your nose, lips, butt, thighs and that little bun you have in the oven is a dead giveaway. Does he know?" Lisa asked.

"I wanted to let everything get back to normal before I told him." Bria responded as she rubbed her baby bump.

"How many months are you? Lisa asked."

"A little over four months." Bria said, looking at her reflection in the mirror.

"That means my niece, or nephew was conceived before the shooting." Lisa stated.

"I had plan to tell him tonight." Bria confessed.

121

"Congratulations!" Lisa quipped.

"So, when do you plan to have a little Rick?" Bria asked jokingly.

"And stretch out this perfect frame, girl I'm not ready for my breast to drop!" Lisa shot back.

"Forget you wench!" Bria said, hurt by her remark.

"I'm sorry honey, let's just pray that motherhood spare your breast." Lisa said, giving her a hug.

"Can we leave now" Bria asked.

"Come on, let's go by Sally's to get some hair, stop and grab something to eat, because I know the baby's hungry, then we can go get our men; okay." Lisa ran off.

"Okay," Bria agreed.

*****

"You think she's going to like it?" Tywoun interrogated.

"I'm sure now just relax, you're about as wired up as a crack-head on the first and the fifteenth." Rick said, with sarcasm.

"I just don't want to do this all wrong." Tywoun replied.

"Trust me man she's going to love; hell, you two might make after tonight." Rick added significance to his statement.

"I can do this, I can do this." Tywoun recited oblivious of Rick's last statement.

Tywoun wasn't quite sure if he could call the queasiness in his stomach butterflies; more like ravenous vultures, the way waves of anxiety recoiled in the pit of his now nauseous stomach. One last glance at the fourteen carat chocolate diamond solitaire; off-set by the luxurious shine of a twenty two carat yellow gold band; accented with princess cuts to add a mysterious level of volume, and he was ready. Closing the Bulgari ring box, Tywoun turned to face Rick before embracing his true friend.

"Thanks Brother. Now let's go, our wives are waiting for us." Tywoun stated, before they exited the jewelry shop.

*****

Back at Rick's house, Lisa and Bria were sitting in the dining area going over seating arrangements and other preparatory issues. When Rick and Tywoun arrived, a rush of confidence told Tywoun what he was about to do was the right thing; and nothing was more important at that moment than to make Bria his wife.

"Bria!" "Tywoun!" They simultaneously called one another.

"Go ahead Queen." Tywoun declared.

"No, you go first Baby." Bria countered.

"Rick, can I see you in here Darling?" Lisa asked, as she was walking to another room.

Alone with Bria, Tywoun searched for that same sense of confidence he not too long ago was filled with as he stared off in Bria's beautiful face.

"Yes Honey?" Bria said, as if to say spit it out.

"You look beautiful tonight; have I told you that lately?" Tywoun asked.

"Every day", Bria responded.

"You look more beautiful tonight. Have you done something different with your hair or your eyes?" Tywoun asked as he examined her facial features, trying to find the right moment to pop the question of all questions.

"Baby, I think I know what you want to ask me." Bria revealed.

Surprised Tywoun inquired, "You do?"

"Yes Baby, I'm pregnant and have known for some time now, please don't be mad at me. I just wanted you to get better before I told you. I was going to tell you tonight, I swear it Baby please don't be mad." Bria said, as she caught her breath.

"No, that's not what I was going to ask" –

"You weren't?" Bria cut him off.

"Wait! Did I just hear you say you're pregnant?" Tywoun asked; Bria's words finally registering.

"A little over four months." Bria said fragilely.

I'm gone be a father again?!" Tywoun shouted excitedly.

"Yes Baby, we're going to be a family!" Bria stated, as she too was overcome by excitement.

"I'm a father, I'm a father, I'm gonna be another father!" Tywoun jumped up and down in the hallway.

"If that wasn't what you were going to ask me, then what were you going to say? Bria questioned.

Reaching into his back pocket, Tywoun retrieved the ring box that was nestled deep in the pocket of his linen shorts. Dropping to one knee; Tywoun took the air from Bria's lungs when he presented her with the most exquisite ring her eyes had ever seen.

"No...No...No..." Bria chanted.

"I haven't asked, and you already shut me down." Tywoun stated, playfully with a big smile.

"Yes...Yes...Yes..." Bria chanted.

"Make your mind up Queen, I still may get a full refund if I get it back before they close." Tywoun joked.

"Ask me...Ask me...Ask me...Baby!"

"Make your mind up." Tywoun teased mercilessly.

"Will you please just ask me?" Bria finally got the words out.

"Bria, I want to spend the rest of my life with you. I want to wipe the boogers out your eyes in the morning. I want to be there looking over you when you get sick, you know feeding you chicken noodles and shit. Baby, I want to be the one to cry your tears when you are sad, and the one you can't stand when you're mad. I guess what I'm trying to say is, Baby – will you marry me?" Tywoun proposed.

"Yes…Yes…Baby, I'll marry you!" Bria shouted, hugging Tywoun lovingly, and kissing him.

"Put it on my finger, Ba!" Bria ordered impatiently.

"You like it?" Tywoun asked.

"I love it, it's beautiful." Bria answered.

"So, you're holding my Lil' Man, huhn?" Tywoun questioned placing his hand on her stomach.

"You mean 'our' Lil' Man, and how you know it ain't 'our' Lil' Momma?" Bria corrected him harmlessly.

"My bad Mrs. Thomas 'our' Love Child." Tywoun restated.

"That sounds better." Bria expressed.

"Look at you two!" Lisa broke in.

"You knew the whole time, Wench, didn't you?" Bria interrogated Lisa with a smile on her face.

"No, just played cupids liaison, me and my partner here. We did good Honey. I can hear the wedding bells now, can't you?" Lisa said, with a big grin.

"So Rick, you were in on this?" Tywoun inquired.

"I think you two make a wonderful couple, how could I not?" Rick replied.

"You two are good." Bria stated.

"Too good," Tywoun seconded.

23 OUT WITH THE OLD; IN WITH THE NEW

"Ladies! Ladies! Can I please have your attention?" Lisa spoke over the commotion in the room." Gather round; Bria stand right here. The rest of y'all please gather round the table, I'd like to make an announcement."

All in attendance circled the V.I.P. room in the expansive Chocolate Factory. Rick and Tywoun felt since this would be the last night of self gratified fulfillment, why not celebrate the symbolic, "coming of an end," in style. Bringing Lisa, Bria, and twenty of their close friends to Orlando for a private viewing of the red hot "Male Review." The night was young, and full of unbridled G-string clad gentlemen, oiled up, and ready to feed their hormonal lust.

"Okay ladies, now that I have your attention, how were your meals? I hope the meal Gladys' catered here tonight was to your liking, there's plenty more so feel free to eat what you like. Well ladies, Bria and I flew you down here to Florida, to share with us, not just our last night of unrestricted fun, but what I as well as my closest friend believes to be the beginning of forever. So, join us as we celebrate. And ladies, do I need to remind you that there are forty of the finest, most toned, caramel, butterscotch, and my favorite sexual dark chocolate Brothers out there right now ready to shake his thang for you just outside this door, and you don't have to share; we have them all to ourselves, but –

"Wooooo!!!" The ladies all erupted. ...but first we have something for you ladies. Fellas, the gifts please." Lisa said, on cue.

Explicit murmurs from the women expressed their delight for the gifts, or the men, who knew?

"Now Pam look at you, and Lynetta; the party ain't even started yet and y'all are already stuffing dollars, y'all are some true hussies!" Lisa stated, all in good fun.

Everyone burst into laughter...

"Bria would you be so kind, and let the ladies know what we've gotten them – please. Pam, girl, you are a trip." Lisa said, as she found her seat.

"Hey all! Lisa and I went to great lengths to prepare a gift we felt fit your very own personality and style. I hope you like Victoria's Secret. Go ahead you can open them. This was just a little something we thought could show our appreciation to all of the friendships we've shared for countless years. Now, what you all have been waiting for, the men are ready for you in the main room. Enjoy, oh, and be safe; and behave!" Bria said, releasing them into the meat factory.

"Woooo!!!" was the sounds of the unabashed women just as the latest rap song blared from the state of the art sound center.

Bria knew that this was going to be one helluva night...

*****

"Fellas, fellas let me have your attention! Tywoun and I would like to welcome you, friends of new and old, to King of Diamonds here in Miami. Tonight gentlemen; just may be the last time we enjoy a night out like this. As you all know, Tywoun and I will be getting married tomorrow to two beautiful women; but how could we NOT spend one more night with our boys?"

"Yeah!!!" they cheered in chorus...

Now listen I know for some of y'all, you'd rather look a gift horse in the mouth than to say, "I do." You may even feel like we're selling out, but you bring a friend to me, as well as Tywoun brought you down here to Miami tonight to show your support – what's that Chris?

"I said, and to watch these beautiful women make it clap."

"Yeah!!! Ssswww..." the men called and whistled like frat brothers...

I'm with you Dog, so I won't hold you guys up any longer. Tywoun is there anything you'd like to say?" Rick asked, passing the torch.

"If all of you would raise your glasses, I'd like to make a toast – here's to love and friendship, and for the countless time we fail trying to balance the two. To love and friendship!" Tywoun saluted.

"Here's to love and friendship!" The room seconded.

"Now get your singles ready, the women are hot, the drinks are on the house, and I heard Malia is in the building along with Esha tonight. Enjoy!" Tywoun said, taking a sip of his very first taste of alcohol.

The scene was frantic. The women were primed and ready to become the object of the impulsive crowd of money totting horn-dogs. Some were fully, and others were semi naked. Beautiful, rotund vixens, all the way down to the bottom of their feet. Whatever your preference, "King of Diamonds" supplied an abundant amount of sexiness. The, premiere strip club in the country, was like shipping for some form of sex inside an old Walmart building.

For Tywoun, this was a new experience, strip clubs were never his cup of tea. Although apprehensive he told himself it would be a perfect opportunity to keep with tradition, and wild out one last time before opting for the more reserved life matrimonial commitment. "What the hell!" He told himself taking another sip of his drink; walking over towards Rick and a few of the guys enjoying the performance taking place on the main stage.

"So, how do you like it so far?" Rick spoke over his shoulder focused on the hypnotic potion of the very limber dancer on stage.

"I feel great, thanks Rick; I mean thanks for everything." Tywoun answered, placing a grateful hand on Rick's shoulder.

"You're welcome Brother, seriously Tywoun I have friends here tonight I've known almost all of my life, but none I hold in more high esteem than you. Congratulations on finding the one thing not worth living without, and its pleasure having you as a friend. Now before I get all mushy, lets savor tonight, because after this – about the only excitement we'll experience will be a first time recipe, or new position in bed. Lets' live in this moment; no holds barred." Rick spoke candidly before reverting his attention back on the show baking a handful of singles.

"No doubt, definitely live in the moment, and by the way, what's the name of the drink you got me?" Tywoun asked with a slight grin on his face, which expressed the enjoyment of the effects of the bubbly inoculant.

"Ace of Spades, you like it?" Rick addressed as he stuck a single in the mouth of the cat crawling dancer that was in front of him.

"It's great." Tywoun responded.

Out of the corner of his eye, Tywoun saw two of the most beautiful women in the building; slowly strutting their way toward him and the guys as if they were walking to the alter.

"Hi, are you Tywoun?" The red boned stallion asked so seductively.

"And you must be Rick?" The more caramel colored beauty stated, more fact than inquiry.

"I'm Tywoun, and to whom do I owe the honor?" He sprinkled the exceptionally gorgeous one with some charm of his own.

"Farika." She replied sensuously with a hint of shyness.

"And my name is Keys-to-the-Cedes." Her co-conspirator spoke with a go getter mentality.

"And may I ask Ms. Cedes why do they call you that?" Rick asked, curiously.

"Well, Honey Bear one taste of my honey, and you gone want to give me the keys to the Mercedes." She invoked a picture of unspoken exploration.

Cedes was the strong know-what-she-wants type, while Farika was the blend of demure promiscuity.

"We hear you two are the soon-to-be grooms, and we want to give you one last night of no-strings-attached pleasure, come with us to the back for a more private intimate dance." Farika said, taking Tywouns hand in hers.

"Yea Daddy, and if you play with me right, I might let you blow my back out." Cedes whispered seductively into Rick's ear, while grabbing a handful of his package.

The dancers led Rick and Tywoun through the dimly lit gentleman's club consumed by a once familiar feeling; lustful craving. Who could blame them, the two dancers were definitely the pick of the litter, fine, stacked, and sexually suggestive. This was a case of the two angels sitting on the shoulders, one is there strictly on logic, while the other more dubious infidel only wanting to entice you with matters of the flesh; annihilating all reasoning. This is where Tywoun and Rick stood as they were placed in the presence of the to-be-or-not-to-be test. The game was called "High Risk", and with four tongue-less walls, and two very enamored vessels driven recklessly on the presumably sweet treat of the forbidden fruit, could be explosive, and yet equally destructive.

*****

"Excuse me Ms., but may I ask why you're sitting over here all alone while the rest of the ladies are no doubt enjoying themselves?" The smooth voice asked from behind.

Bria was busted; she truly thought she had found her a safe haven. Unlike the other women, she just wanted to enjoy the male dancers from afar. The last thing she wanted was to have some total stranger shaking his junk all up in her face. Besides, she was wondering what Tywoun was doing at their bachelor party. She glanced over the message that she had just completed on her i-Phone to send to Tywoun, hoping that he wasn't too busy to read it. She pressed the send button on her phone then placed it back into her clutch purse, before she turned her head to politely decline the offer of a dance so she thought.

"I'm sorry, but I was just - , she paused surprised to find a Shamar Moore looking brother fully clothed standing there patiently – Oh, you're not a"

"Dancer," he finished before her.

"Yes, that's what I was going to say." Bria replied.

"No, I'm sorry I'm not, but if you want I could get you one." He came back with a little humor breaking the ice.

"No, no – I wasn't saying like I was wanting one. I was just glad to see that you had all your clothes on." Bria responded gratefully.

"Apologies, I am D'von," he introduced.

"Hi D'von, my name is Bria," she accepted his introduction by shaking his hand.

"Ms. Bria would you mind me asking if it would be alright if I'd join you?" D'von asked humbly.

"I was really trying to be alone, but I guess I could use some conversation." Bria answered reluctantly.

"Wonderful!" D'von expressed taking the seat in front of Bria.

"Excuse me for asking, but what is a nice looking man like you doing in a male strip club, you're not gay are you? Not that I'm against gays, it's just I was wondering." Bria asked fumbling over her words.

"No, please it's no harm. I can understand why you would ask that question, being that this is a gentleman's club. To answer your question, I am a heterosexual, I love women with passion. There, comfortable now?" D'von stated giving Bria a hard time.

"I didn't mean it like that; please don't feel offended." Bria tried using damage control.

"I'm just giving you a hard time. Honestly, I would have asked the same question if I were you. So, again, it's no harm." D'von assured Bria.

"Well D'von do you mind if I ask what are you doing here – you're not one of those desperate guys that like to pick up women after their hormones have been stirred up by all of the humping and pumping going on in here, are you?" Bria interrogated adding a little of her own humor.

"Ha, you're not only fine, you're also funny." D'von stated as he laughed at her jestering.

"Fill a sister in." Bria quipped feeling more comfortable in his presence.

"Seriously, I'm the owner. I just wanted to come down a quick minute from my office to make sure everything and everyone was okay. I noticed you sitting alone, so; I thought I would check in on you to see if you were displeased with something within the club." D'von said, delivering a warm smile.

"I hate to kill your flow, but I'm getting married tomorrow, and I am loyal to my man. So there's not much more I can offer you." Bria laid her boundaries.

"So, you're one of the brides, congratulations, and just to let you know,

I'm happily married myself." D'von relayed as he showed off his wedding band.

"I'm sorry, I thought you were trying to come on to me, I see I've managed to stick my foot in my mouth again!" Bria said embarrassed.

"You seem to be making it a habit. Please, it would be nice to just share a candid conversation with a beautiful woman like Ms. Bria." D'von revealed his truest intentions.

"What would you like to talk about?" Bria questioned.

"First, may I order you a drink that I'm sure you will love it?" D'von offered.

"I can't drink tonight." Bria responded.

"You are old enough aren't you?" D'von interrogated sarcastically.

"You're inquisition is quite flattering, but I assure you, age isn't the reason." Bria stated smiling.

"Humor me." D'von insisted.

"I'm expecting." Bria stated, bluntly.

"Again, congratulations. I have just the perfect drink for you...Waitress!"

...

"Yes Mr. Davis?" the fresh face waitress responded.

"May I please have a double shot of Nuevo, and an ice water, and for the lady a Passion Fruit Hurricane, thank you?" D'von smiled as he placed his order with the waitress.

"Will that be all Sir?" the waitress asked.

"Yes Ma'am." D'von said, dismissingly.

"So tell me Mr. Davis how long have you been married?" Bria asked.

"I've been with my wife for sixteen years, but in the eye of the courts it's been six years by law."

"So after ten years you realized you didn't want to live without her?" Bria went on to ask as if feeling his wife's frustration.

"I've known since day one that my life would be better with Wanda by my side. It's just we both went on to get our P.H.D.'s, and with the both of us attending universities across the country; I was studying abroad as a Rhodes Scholar, we both decided to wait before we made that final commitment. We wanted to make sure we really loved one another." D'von spoke so passionately.

"That's sweet." Bria stated.

"What's even sweeter is that we formed a true unconditional love for one another, due to the fact that time, or distance never dulled the potency on the spell love enraptured us in, because; we were very determined individuals.

It is true Bria that love's secret lies in the moments where temptation is outweighed by loyalty, and no way will you betray the unseen eyes of the one you love." D'von spoke with sincerity.

"You're really a gentleman I see." Bria stated as she instantly gained a new level of respect for D'von.

"Here's your double shot of Nuevo Mr. Davis, and your Passion Fruit Hurricane Ms. – enjoy," the waitress cut in their conversation while placing their orders in front of them.

"Thanks! This is a non-alcoholic beverage right?" Bria questioned suspiciously circling the chilled drink under her nose.

"I'm hurt you would think that I would do such a thing." D'von stated, shocked.

"I don't know, a smooth talker like you, one never can be too sure," Bria said, raising an unsure eyebrow.

"So now I'm a serial killer plotting to abduct you, drive you out to some unknown remote area, have my way with you, and then kill you. Let me see, is that who I am?" D'von stated lightheartedly.

"Look, you are a fine, educated, black brother, who seems to love your wife more than life itself, and you're well mannered – you might just be a serial killer." Bria smiled taking a sip of her drink as she winked away her concern.

*****

"…Tonight we'll be making love faces – Making love faces – Shadows on the wall while the candles burning – Messing up the bed while I'm sweating out your perm…" were the words coming off a Trey Songz CD as Farika was in a trance as she worked her voluptuous backside to the rhythm of the song.

Tywoun was overwhelmed by the sultry seductress that was dancing in front of him, he could no longer ignore the urge to touch what was before him that looks to be so soft.

"Oohh, Daddy, yes touch it again. It's so soft ain't it Daddy?" Farika said, as she rolled her tongue inside of her mouth so enticingly.

"Like cotton candy." Tywoun replied lost in her voluptuous curves.

"Daddy I like when you touch me, it erupts a burning sensation through my body – don't stop – touch me more." Farika whined.

Lustful thoughts raced through Tywoun's head as Farika stood in front of him, working her body as if she was a snake in motion. Tywoun was stuck as if he was putty in her hands. Tipsy, Tywoun's inhibitions were down, and his little head was beginning to think for him more and more. Farika understood

Tywoun was totally tune into her, she gently mounted herself onto his lap. Once comfortable with her seating arrangement, she immediately started gyrating her hot box against him for the sole purpose of bringing him to a full erection.

"Kiss my neck, now go down my breast, sss… put one in your mouth that feels so good – yes, don't stop. Oooo Baby…Ahh…I feel you Daddy coming through shorts; can I see what you're working with?" Farika whispered into Tywoun's ear before she started sucking on his earlobe with her warm mouth.

In one fluid motion, Farika slithered herself onto her knees as she delicately unzipped Tywoun's feather weight linen shorts exposing a bulge under his white cotton briefs he had on.

"Fine and packing. Baby we're going to make a movie tonight." Farika stated with a huge smile on her face.

After a few soft kisses to his naval, Farika reached into Tywoun's underwear pulling every inch of him out, letting his lower self-join the party.

"Oooo Daddy, I like what I see and I want it." Were the words that Farika stated before placing Tywoun's manhood deep into her wet mouth?

Tywoun howled at the moon like a lost dog as he tried to control his breathing as he fought the urge of wanting to relieve himself. Farika was a beast, she knew how to work her magic, unfolding one trick after another. All Tywoun could do was sit and enjoy the pleasure he was receiving.

"Ahhhhh…" Tywoun cried out totally taken by the current fantasy that had become so true.

Putting a bottle of champagne to his lips preparing to take a drink.

"Daddy what's this hard thing in your pocket? Can you move it for me; it's messing my groove up." Farika requested as she came up for some air.

"Yea, that's my phone let me get it for you." Tywoun replied.

"That's better Daddy, now I can please you much better; grab my ass Daddy, I like the way you handle it," and then she placed his manhood back into her mouth.

Tywoun took a quick glance at his phone screen; seeing an unread text, he quickly touched the screen to see it was from Bria. Tywoun sat up instantly.

"That feels good to you Daddy?" Farika whispered.

Tywoun sobered up as he started to read the text Bria sent him…

"I miss you Ty-Ty, I'd rather be making love to you right now, than be stuck here. I love you…"

Tywoun thought about what he was doing; damn I'm supposed to be getting married tomorrow to the woman I love and I'm letting a pro slob on my knob which truly belongs to my wife-to-be. Tywoun instantly broke from his thoughts and the spell that Farika had him under.

"I can't continue with this, we have to stop." Tywoun commanded.

"Yes you can Daddy, let me drink you up." Farika replied, ignoring his wishes.

"No…you have to stop, seriously." Tywoun stood firm.

"You're serious?!" Farika said, as she displayed disappointment on her face.

"I'm supposed to be getting married tomorrow, and I'm here with you – there's nothing wrong with you. I just read my wife-to-be message on my phone and she stated that she was just sitting at her bachelorette party wishing she could be making love to me." Tywoun said, as he stood up to fasten his pants.

"Suga, I hope she's worth it, because my pussy is hot like a pipe bomb." Farika promoted as she patted her hot spot.

"One day you'll understand when you find that special one truly for you."

"Let me fix myself up, and I'll walk you back up front." Farika stated as she fastened her bra.

Tywoun stopped at the private room Rick and Cedes occupied, tapping on the door a couple of times before opening the door.

"Yo Rick, I'm heading back to the hotel." Tywoun stated.

Rick was having a blast. A bottle of Ace of Spades in one hand, and a handful of singles in the other. He was truly enjoying the show Cedes was performing in the middle of the floor.

"Yo Ty, you and Farika come on and join the party." Rick hollered over the music.

"I'm good Rick, I'm going to call it a night. I had enough fun for the night. If you want me, I'll be at the hotel." Tywoun said, turning to the door to walk out.

"Alright Ty! Farika come on and start dancing for me Baby Girl, let me see you make it clap!" Rick said, as he took another sip of his drink.

*****

The time rolled by it seemed; effortlessly for Bria. Being in the presence of D'von helped bide her time over until the other women were ready to go back to the hotel. D'von was very insightful, and ushered Bria through their conversation with the utmost respect. He never over stepped his boundaries, and more importantly he knew how to listen. There were several qualities Bria identified in him that helped her believe D'von was a good man, good husband, and a good business man. Maybe in another lifetime Bria could see herself being attracted to a man such as D'von. But this was an uncertainty better not thought about, because who knows if reincarnation is actual, and her heart beat only for the oncoming moments to be shared with the one she unquestionably loved. She thought was it wrong for her to enjoy another man's company in this form, or was she foolish, if believing the law attraction only kicks in when and only when in the presence of a preordained being cut from a one of a kind cloth?

"D'von let me ask you; how do you deal with the temptation?" Bria queried.

"Are you hitting on me?" D'von asked, jokingly.

"Stop, I'm serious." Bria said, with a straight face.

"That's the best question you've asked tonight. Let's see hmm…Allow it to consume you, bringing you right to the point of crossing that line. Then ask yourself these two questions: Can this decision outweigh everything in your life? And: …Why can't I lust over the one I love? I can almost guarantee nothing will bring you to answering these questions yes." D'von replied, as honest as he could.

"I really like that, good answer." Bria confessed.

"Use it. Now I hate to leave this conversation, but I promised Wanda that I'd be in by midnight. So if you would excuse me, I better be going. It was nice meeting you Bria, and I wish you and Tywoun many blessings. I hope he's worthy of such an astounding woman such as you. Again, thanks for the conversation. Good night, and God be with you," were the closing words from D'von as he extended his hand when he stood up.

"The pleasure was all mine. Thank you and it was nice meeting you too. Goodnight and don't keep Wanda waiting, go give her the loving she deserves." Bria replied.

Once again, Bria found herself sitting alone, this time she begin to play-back the conversation D'von and her had just shared; storing the wonderful tidbits that D'von had shared about keeping the romance alive, and fully functional.

"Here you are, I've been looking all over for you Ms. Hussy, and here you are sitting over here by yourself. Are you ready to go? The girls and I are ready to go." Lisa said, obviously tipsy and tired.

"I thought you'd never ask. Let me check my messages, and go use the girls' room." Bria said, as she retrieved her phone out of her clutch purse.

"Now Bria let him enjoy himself you will have him for the rest of your life." Lisa spoke with a slight slur.

"He texted me back, and he – wait. Why is he saying he is sorry? I'm sorry Baby, tonight I almost gave in to temptation, but I'm back at the room, the guys just made it in. I'll explain later…I love you!" Bria read aloud.

Bria guessed what D'von shared with her concerning temptation was true. Which made her appreciate his conversation even more.

"Come on Hussy, I'm ready to go." Lisa demanded.

"Alright with your drunk ass. Come on Wench, we have a wedding later on today, let's get some sleep…

24 REAL LOVE WITHSTANDS IT ALL

Bria and Lisa along with the bride's maids and a few other friends boarded the hotel shuttle bus to their awaiting luxurious private jet heading to Miami.

Upon arriving in Miami, they were greeted, then whisked off by a personalized glam squad so they all could receive total make overs.

Once they arrived to their destination there was no delays in starting to transform the ladies into greater beauty. It was like they were placed on a conveyor belt; the first station was to get shampooed and conditioned. The next station was for Mani's and Pedi's, after, they were to receive signature hair styling. Once done, they would have to be clothed into their ceremony dresses.

The scenery for the wedding was sure to be a breath taker, it was architecture by the world renowned Gitta of "Gitta's Fabulous Wedding Planning & Ceremonies." After many hours of consultation with the couples to be married; Gitta decided on making the wedding theme color vanilla crème and raspberry sorbet. The colors complemented the subtle complexions of Bria and Rick, and the more robust shadings of Tywoun and Lisa. Gitta also went a little further by adding a barrage of carnations, lilies, and a giant dragon breath wreath as the centerpiece. The women would be donning a Romona Keveza chiffon and lace strapless hip-hugging ensemble. Bria and Lisa both had three-fourth quarter length extensions to their gowns. Along with a provocative split that reached the side of their hips for an extra sex appeal. While in the dressing room, the women practiced their best cat walk, inserting a little fun into the tense, but yet inviting atmosphere.

"Girl, I'm glad I got that Brazilian wax." Bria said, in good humor.

"Tell me about it, my man is going to need a clear path down there tonight." Lisa replied.

"You're a mess" Bria shot back.

"A mess is what I'm trying to leave; you hear me!? Lisa said, as she received high fives from the other women in the room that agreed with her statement.

*****

When the men finally got up from last night's hangovers, they all met downstairs in the banquet room where they enjoyed one last brunch of, 'just us boys.' It was the coming of age, and all the men shared their thoughts of encouragement, and they let it be known that if all else failed, the brothers would always be around if they needed them in anyway. Rick and Tywoun presented the pack with 18 karat gold Rolexes commemorating the bond that never was to be broken; regardless of the situation they were a band of brothers. The growth and maturity in the room was accepted, and supported by one and all.

After the presentation of the gifts, and the sharing of words, they enjoyed brunch prepared for them. The menu consisted of steak, eggs and Belgium waffles.

After they finished eating, new haircuts from Montay, Jaelen, and BJ who were all licensed barbers, was given; and a part of the pack. After getting the cuts complete, they went back to their rooms to make final preparations before heading to the cathedral for the main event.

When the men arrived, they were ushered into a dressing room where their Italian cut tuxedoes designed by Versace were placed and awaited them to change into. When everyone had changed into their attire, their appearance was like mannequins. They gave each other dap and complimented each other.

There was only ten minutes left before vows would be exchanged and a new chapter of love would begin for Rick and Tywoun. The sounds of family and friends were filling the pews could be heard lingering down the halls into the dressing room.

"Five minutes from now, you and I will be married men; are you ready my brother?" Rick asked, as he straightened Tywoun's novicely tied tie.

"I can't wait to see Bria. I know she's going to look so beautiful, man." Tywoun said, as Rick was putting the final touches to his tie.

"I'll let you know now, you get two minutes to let the tears flow. No harassment, I promise." Rick replied, felicity as he completed his work on Tywouns' tie.

"You just better hope you can cut them off in two minutes," Tywoun responded.

"…Gentlemen, we will be starting momentarily, so could everyone start taking their positions," the service-men announced.

"No turning back now." Tywoun stated.

"You have the rings?" Rick questioned.

"Right here my brother." Tywoun replied, taking one last look at them before passing them to their best men.

*****

"…Ladies, the men are getting in position right now. We'll be starting within five minutes," the elderly service-woman announced.

"Bri the rest of our lives starts now. You've been my best friend since break-dancing, and big hair-dos. I just want you to know you've helped me through my pain, and got me to see that Rick could free my heart which I had incarcerated. I love you, my friend and sister. Thank you!" Lisa said, as she fought back her tears.

"And it was because of you that made me willing to seek love again, so much of my heart was confined by loneliness. Thank You! Now, let's go marry our men." Bria said, placing her hand in Lisa's as the two exited the dressing room into the hallway.

At the end of the corridor sat Bria's God Father who would assume the duties of giving the both of them away, in the absence of their biological fathers. Just past him was a packed house of family and friends. At the end of the alter Tywoun and Rick, along with their groomsmen stood waiting looking extremely handsome. The ravishing bridesmaids took their places, adding a much needed feminine quality to the arch of men. Brittani and Elise were so cute, Brittani was the ring bearer and Elise was the official flower girl; they looked so sweet in their matching dresses. Seeing them made Bria even prouder, because she knew their mother Sharice was seated near her family to show her support and approval.

On cue, the organist strummed the first cord setting in motion the blessed engagement. Bria's godfather took his place between the two beautiful soon-to-be brides, and proudly allowed them to take an arm as he proceeded to escort them down the aisle. Bria and Lisa were amazed at how handsome the men were. Those in attendance smiled and were happy they were able to be a part of such a special occasion as witnesses to their impending nuptials.

Coming to the end of what seemed to be the longest walk of their lives; Bria and Lisa joined their grooms at the altar. All you saw from the four of them were smiles as they waited to recite their vows to one another, which would hold them obligated to a simplistic 'I do.'

"Wow! Bria you-you look wonderful!" Tywoun said, in awe of her beauty.

"Thank you, you look very handsome yourself!" Bria replied smiling from ear to ear.

"Lisa, damn baby you look good." Rick stated.

"Wait til you see me without my clothes on…forgive me Jesus." Lisa whispered in Rick's ear.

The time had come to start the ceremony.

"Lord, heavenly Father we have gathered here today to join in the union between man and woman. These two young couples have found love by following the blue-print of your design. Rick and Lisa would you two like to exchange your vows first?

"They both said, spontaneously 'Yes'!"

"Rick, I haven't stopped smiling since you came into my life. You have opened my heart and filled it with an unbelievable love. It is you I crave when confronted by hunger, and it's you that bring purpose to my life. As wife, I vow to honor your name, cherish your presence and give back unconditionally the love you so generously give to me. I just want to thank you for loving me so unselfishly, and for truly freeing my incarcerated heart…" Lisa ended dabbing the tears away.

"Lisa take me to new heights. Journey to new lands with me. Let's live without restrictions. I want you to know you can look uncertainty in the eyes fearlessly; knowing I'll be there. Share with me when you are mad. Allow me to comfort you when you're sad, and when the time is right, let me show you that I can be a wonderful dad. My love for you Lisa will not be graded by the moments we are happy together, but by the unforeseen moments where we get on each other's nerves, yet refuse to walk away. This is my vow to you. Take my heart and my love will follow." Rick spoke reaching to wipe a tear from Lisa's cheek.

"…And now for you two."

"I dreamed of you many nights, as I laid alone in my bed. Never could I have dreamt I would find you standing right before my eyes. For you to have stepped out from the shadows of your past to embrace responsibility is admirable. You are the missing piece to my puzzle, and I love the picture I see when you're in it. My love, my life – the father of our unborn child. As your wife, I will serve you, and as a mother, I will love and protect our child with my life. Because I love you, I love your girls as though they're my own. They've brought so much joy to my life and unbeknownst to them, they've helped prepare me for mother hood. This is my vow to you, for releasing my heart which was once incarcerated…" Bria recited gracefully.

"Just eight months ago I wasn't sure where I'd be, but to earn the right to be a father to my children, and to find a love that I could call my own was what I've been praying for. I'm proud to say my children are here today. Hi Brittani, Hi Elise. I'm equally proud to be in love with a wonderful woman like you. Bria, as your husband I vow to praise, protect, and provide for you and our child/children. Believe in me. I will never deceive you…" Tywoun states, as tears filled his eyes.

"Lisa Denise Hamilton, do you vow to love, honor and cherish Rick Avery Moss through thick and thin; in sickness and health, until death you do part?"

"I do!" Lisa answered.

"Rick Avery Moss, do you vow to love, honor and cherish Lisa Denise Hamilton through thick and thin; in sickness and in health? Until death you do part?"

"I do! Rick spoke clearly."

"Bria Michelle Lewis, do you vow to love, honor and cherish Tywoun Tyrell Thomas through thick and thin; in sickness and in health? Until death you do part?"

"I do!" Bria replied, as she smiled.

"Tywoun Tyrell Thomas, do you vow to love, honor and cherish Bria Michelle Lewis through thick and thin; in sickness and in health? Until death you do part?"

"I do!" Tywoun answered.

Lisa, Rick, Bria and Tywoun; I ask that you all now exchange your rings with one another.

"By the power invested in me, I now pronounce you all husbands and wives. You guys may now salute your brides."

The audience erupted when the two couples embraced in the first of many long, passionate kisses.

*****

At the Ritz's Expo Center the party was about to begin as everyone gathered around the newly-weds to witness the cutting of the wedding cake. The cake was a beautiful four tier chocolate hazelnut cake. The couples feed each other a piece of the cake before it became open season to the guests. Once they shared the first dance, the party began.

Photos were being taking in adjoining rooms as well as in the outside gazebo. Both couples wanted to capture all the special moments of this blessed event.

Sharice approached Bria and Tywoun while Brittani and Elise ran around playing with all the other children.

"Congratulations!" Sharice stated.

"Thank you, Sharice." Bria responded.

"I'm glad you made this trip, thank you for allowing our girls to be a part of our special day." Tywoun said, giving Sharice a quick hug.

"We're family, how could I miss this, and what's the word on the baby; is it going to be a boy or girl?" Sharice asked with a sincere smile.

"We're waiting until we get back from the honeymoon to find out the sex." Bria replied.

"Have fun, enjoy yourselves. Let me go congratulate the other newly-weds, I'll talk to you two later." Sharice said as she walked away.

"Thanks again Sharice." Bria stated.

"We have an hour before we are to board the cruise ship to start our honeymoon, but first, may I have this dance?" Tywoun asked with an outstretched hand.

"I thought you'd never ask." Bria answered; let's show Rick and Lisa how to really step as she laughed..

25 HAPPY ENDINGS

As the cruise ship sailed carelessly through the tropic waters of the Atlantic, Bria, Tywoun, Lisa and Rick sat on the top deck looking out at the endless miles of the sea. The ambience of the night sky was amplified by the clarity of stars strung along as if placed there by the splatter of an artist's brush. The view was beautiful. With the exception of Bria, the others shared a bottle of Dom Perignon. Bria enjoyed a glass of chilled grape juice.

"Well guys, this is it – here's to love, family and happiness." Rick toasted.

"To love, family and happiness, "Lisa repeated.

"And a night full of passion." Tywoun chimed in.

"A night, why not for life?" Bria corrected with a smirk.

With that being said, the couples retired to their executive cabins where not only did they consummate their marriages, but they unlocked the secrets of their love as husband and wife.......

ABOUT THE AUTHOR

Born from a bloodline of royalty and slavery, an established warrior from the womb, blessed with the heart of a lion and a back made of steel. A true southern go-getter with a charm that could get a peach tree to hand over its' fruit. Yes, a true Knoxvillian!

Interested in our services? Want to purchase books available through us? Visit us at www.afmpublishers.com No access to the web? Email us at afmpublishers@gmail.com.

Coming Soon:

- **Prison Fantasies**
An AFM Publications collaboration

- **City Under Siege (Trilogy)**
By A. R. Mwamba

- **Gittin' It Young**
Wollo's Son and new Author Fallon

www.ingramcontent.com/pod-product-compliance
Lightning Source LLC
Chambersburg PA
CBHW071947170626
46813CB00005B/1859